Rocker From the Rez

Lance Chalmers

Print ISBNs

Amazon print 9780228628309
Ingram Spark 9780228628316
BWL Print 9780228628323

BWL Publishing

Books we love to write ...
Authors around the world.

http://bwlpublishing.ca

Dedication

For Louis and Mary Bates, and my entire Cree family. And for my mother, Anne Chalmers, who through her knowledge and guidance kept me rooted in my Cree heritage.

Table of Contents

"There can never be peace between nations until there is first known that true peace which is within the souls of men." – Black Elk

Chapter 1

A strong gale whistles through the branches of the snow-covered pines. I stuff my hands into the shallow pockets of my worn jean jacket and continue to push against the cold Manitoba wind.

Mabel walks out of her house just as I'm passing her front steps. Despite the snapping cold, she's smiling. "Hey, Ray. Are you going to the lodge?"

I nod as she hurries to match my pace.

"Where's Donna?" she says.

"Mom's already at the lodge."

Mabel nods. "You know, I think she misses ya now that you've moved off the rez."

I shrug. "There's far too many people crammed into houses here. I need to concentrate on my music without someone banging on the front door or calling every five minutes."

As soon as we round the corner of the road, I see four people gathering in front of the lodge, smoking. Mabel briefly speaks to them as I walk up and open the heavy wooden door. As we walk in, a waft of warm air greets us, carrying with it a welcoming aroma of sage.

At the centre of the big room are chairs arranged in a large circle. Most of the people in the village are here—a good turnout considering the weather. Mabel pats me on the back, then points to where my mother is sitting. I find my way over to her and sit down in the empty chair she was obviously saving for me.

She smiles and leans in close. "I'm glad you made it. I was starting to worry you had changed your mind." Then, she looks me up and down. "Where is your winter coat? Why would you go out in this weather wearing nothing but an Indian tuxedo?"

Indian tuxedo—a jean jacket, a term coined by some of the locals. "I'm fine. I'm pretty sure I'm acclimatized after being raised here."

Just then, the door to the office opens and in walks the Chief, Harlan Brown, and two women clothed in traditional beaded dresses. The chatter in the room comes to a slow halt as the chief and the women join the circle.

The chief thanks everyone for coming, then gets down to business. He covers a handful of recent issues—garbage had been strewn all over the rez by wild animals due to someone's carelessness—then addresses the complaints about loud music played too late at night. Thankfully I'm no longer to blame for this, having moved off the rez.

After all the menial issues are dealt with, he announces the main reason the meeting was called—the vision quest.

"Soon, when the snow has cleared, we have two young men who will embark on their personal journey to find enlightenment and self-awareness, and to find their connection with Mother Earth."

My mother leans in close again. "You know, it's not too late for you. You're only in your twenties. A lot of men go on their vision quest when they're older."

"I'm not old, and just because I haven't gone doesn't mean I don't appreciate our traditions."

She leans in even closer. "Yes. It kind of does. Don't you think that people in the village wonder about you, especially since you moved off the rez?"

I sigh deeply. "I told you, I don't care what people say. I am being true to myself by following my own journey."

The chief discusses how the two boys will be mentored in preparation for their vision quest, and how all the residents should be supportive and proud.

Everyone in the large circle claps, especially my mother. She makes sure she's the loudest, to emphasize her point.

When the meeting ends, everyone filters out of the lodge. Funnels of airborne snow swirl around us as Mom and I make our way toward the house.

By the time we arrive, our faces and hands are bright red and numb. I take a seat at the kitchen table as Mom puts the kettle on. She grabs two cups from the cupboard and fills them with the steaming hot water, then drops a teabag in each before joining me at the table. "Are you staying for dinner?"

I shake my head. "I can't. As soon as I get home, me and the guys are going to rehearse. We have a gig coming up in Flin Flon this weekend. We need to put as much time as we can into practicing."

Mom asks me how things are going with the band. I reassure her that we're working more than most groups are right now, though we're still barely able to cover the rent and bills every month.

"Why is that?"

"Mostly, it's been because of Butch."

"What about Butch?"

"He drinks too much on the road, and by the end of the night he starts wrecking shit in the bar. When we go to get paid, they charge us for whatever he broke."

Mom shakes her head. "I always knew he was no good. So did everyone else in the village. I don't know why you let him stay in the band. Didn't you tell me that he's not even a good musician?"

"Yeah. He's not. I think if he practiced or showed up for rehearsals he would do okay, but he just doesn't have the interest. As far as why I don't tell him to take a hike, it's hard. We all grew up with him. I was waiting for him to change. But as far as we can see, that's not happening."

"You can't keep him in the band. Not if it's costing you money and your reputation. How long do you think your agent can keep booking you with him acting out?"

"I know. The rest of us have talked about it. If he messes up at the Flin Flon gig, he's out. We already have another bass player waiting to take his spot."

"Good! You've worked so hard to get your band up and playing. It would be a shame to have it destroyed by someone like Butch, who only cares about himself."

After visiting a while, I get up from the table to leave. Before I can make it to the door, my mother reminds me of the powwow scheduled to take place in April. "You should put your name in to be a drummer. So many people will be there, and I think it would show the chief that even though you live off the rez, you're still part of the community."

I sigh and shake my head. "I know how much you want me to stay connected to the village and our traditions, but I have so little spare time. I can't promise anything. I can only tell you that I will try."

11

* * *

When I reach the house, I hear that the boys are already rehearsing. However, one notable instrument is missing. I walk inside, hang up my jacket, and head to the back bedroom we dedicated as our rehearsal space.

Already into the second verse of Blackwater Jack, one of our original tunes, Joe and Adrian nod at me as I take a seat at my kit and chime in. Once the song is finished, Joe turns around to face me. "How the hell can we practice as a band without Butch here to play bass? This is bullshit, Ray. Every time we set a time, he always comes up with some lame-ass excuse for ditching." Joe's brown eyes look even darker now, and his brows are furrowed.

Just as I'm about to answer, Adrian butts in. "Yeah, man. This is stupid. Either we get rid of Butch or I'm out."

I shrug. "I know. Don't you think I feel the same way? I've put everything into this band. I don't know what the hell Butch is up to, I just know that his priorities are all messed up. Still, we did agree to let him play the Flin Flon gig. And he knows that if he fucks up there, he's out. No questions asked."

Adrian shakes his head, making the small hairs of his newly styled mohawk sway. "All right, Ray. But if he screws up another gig, don't go soft on him again. This story is getting old fast."

"I won't. I promise. I mean, we all grew up with him, and I guess I believed when he said he was dedicated to the band. I really hoped focusing on something productive like music would distract him from drinking and fighting all the time."

Joe scoffs. "Not likely. He's been the same way since seventh grade. He's had a lot of years to grow into the fuck-up he is."

Adrian laughs. "It's the only thing he's ever been good at."

We do our best to get through the setlist without the bass. Once we're finished, the three of us go to the kitchen and are just about to make dinner when there's a rap at the front door, followed by the awkward sounds of Butch walking in.

Adrian glares at him. "Why don't you wait for someone to answer the door. You don't live here, or pay rent—"

"Yeah," Joe interrupts. "And thanks for showing up for practice."

Butch feigns surprise. "Oh, no. I thought we were rehearsing tomorrow night. Shit, man. Sorry. And I was going to stop by earlier, but there was a lodge meeting on the rez."

I shake my head. "Nice try. I was there, and I didn't see you anywhere."

Butch's eyes widen. "Oh. Were you there? I, um...I got there late because my

Aunty Josie needed help getting wood. I must've just missed you."

I'm about to respond to his bullshit story but realize there's no point. No matter what I say, he'll have some bullshit story to counteract it.

He does his best to change the subject. "So, what's for dinner?"

No matter how irritated we all are with Butch, we know how poor he is. Even if we're skint on food, we always feed him when he's here.

After making a quick mixture of hamburger, Kraft dinner and canned tomatoes, the four of us sit in the living room and watch Bonanza reruns as we eat. During a commercial, Joe brings up the gig. "So, is the hotel booked for this weekend?"

I nod. "Yeah. I took care of that yesterday."

Joe turns his attention to Butch. "And what about you? Are you going to show up on time?"

Butch scoffs. "Of course, man. I'll be here early. Hell, if you want, I can even come over the day before and stay the night."

"No," the rest of us say in unison.

"Just don't screw up this gig, Butch," Joe continues. "They treat us good, and they pay well, too."

The show comes back on, taking the attention off Butch.

After an hour I get up, wash my dish in the sink, and head to my room. As I lie quietly on my bed, I hear Butch ask Joe and Adrian if they want to call the bootlegger for a bottle. I can't hear their answer, but I'm positive neither of them wants to drink, especially with a guy who turns into an animal after only a couple of drinks. Soon after, I hear the front door slam, then the sounds of Adrian and Joe heading to their rooms. I think their tolerance for Butch is waning fast.

Chapter 2

It's Friday morning. After a long couple of rehearsal days, we're ready to pack up the van and head to Flin Flon. Much to our surprise, Butch actually shows up on time.

The first stretch of the journey is rough, with deep snow covering the two-lane highway. At one point I have to slow to 30kmh until the white-out recedes.

Both Joe and Adrian are sleeping in the back seat with their heads resting against the windows, leaving me with only Butch to talk with. For the next few hours, he goes on and on about a young girl on the rez by the name of Dakota, and how different she is from every other female in the village. "She's not only the most beautiful girl I've ever seen on the reservation, but she's fun, too. While I was following her and her friends to the river, everyone was too afraid to walk over the rapids on a log. Everyone but Dakota. She almost slipped and went headfirst into the water, but instead of screaming, she just laughed. She's my kind of girl. Brave and daring."

I nod absently, until something alarming he said resurfaces in my mind. "What do you mean, you *followed* them? Did they know you were there?"

Butch scoffs. "C'mon, man. Don't act like a Dudley Do-Right. Don't tell me you've never followed someone you liked."

I shake my head and briefly take my eyes off the slippery road to look at him. "Never."

He laughs, then playfully punches me on the arm. "Maybe you should've been a cop instead of a musician."

I want to share my disgust about why stalking someone is so wrong, but I know whatever I say will disappear in that empty head of his. Instead, I turn on the radio and listen for the road report.

* * *

Flin Flon has a population of around five-thousand and is located on the border of Saskatchewan and Manitoba. The people here are hard-working, mostly blue collar, and very welcoming to strangers. Every time I've been here, I've taken away warm memories. When I turned eight, my father bought me a camera and my mother and him brought me here to the wildlife sanctuary to take pictures of the animals—one of my fondest memories I have that includes my dad.

As I pull up to the hotel, I tap the brakes and jerk the van to wake up Joe and Adrian.

After we file into the small lobby and check in, the four of us decide to go down the street to the small diner for a bite to eat.

During the meal, Butch promises that while we're playing in Flin Flon for the next two nights, he won't drink a drop. Joe and Adrian roll their eyes in disbelief; we've all heard it before.

Thankfully we all ordered the special, leaving us just enough money to eat until we get paid after the gig.

When we're finished at the small eatery, we drive to the venue and set up our gear. Barney, the house soundman, is glad to see us and offers to buy a round of beer. As much as Adrian, Ray and I could use a cold drink, especially when it's free, we gracefully decline so we don't encourage Butch. Barring the odd occasion, none of us are drinkers except for him.

Butch has lost over half of his immediate family from booze. His brother, Randy, is doing life for killing someone in a drunken brawl, his father died of kidney disease, and one of his sisters drowned in her own vomit while passed out—she was fifteen years old. You would think that these huge losses would put him off booze forever, but for whatever reason, it only made him worse.

My mom is right—most people on the rez don't like Butch. They think he's got a few screws loose for how he carries on fighting and destroying people's property. Even in grade school, he was trouble. He was always in the principal's office for fighting. No one was brave enough to challenge him, and the majority of the scraps were when he targeted some poor kid and bullied the shit out of him.

I'm not sure why I never turned tail and dumped him as a friend. I suppose I felt sorry for him. Maybe a part of me was scared to ignore him. He's never taken rejection well.

* * *

The bar is already packed when we walk in. On our way to the stage, the bar manager, an elderly fellow who always wears sweater vests, approaches us. He thanks us for coming, then asks if we could play an Elvis song because he brought his wife and she's a huge fan. Then he tells us that when we take our breaks, all appetizers are on him. I wish all bar managers were this kind. I promise him a good show and agree to his request of playing an Elvis tune before continuing to the stage.

We play the first set as well as possible, especially considering Butch has missed so many rehearsals, but the crowd loves us. Not only were they cheering after every song, but the small dance floor was also packed, which definitely makes us look good to the manager and will help ensure we get asked back.

On our first break, the four of us head to the back room to get away from the noise in the bar. As soon as we sit down, there's a knock on the door and a barmaid walks in with a tray of hot wings.

Joe delves into the wings. "This is probably the best club we play. I wish all our gigs were this packed."

"The better we get, the more word of mouth will reach other clubs and we'll get better gigs," I say. "Probably more money, too."

Butch stands up, slides his phone out of his pocket, then walks to the door. "I'm going outside to try and get a hold of Dakota." He grins before leaving the room.

Joe looks at me. "Who the hell is Dakota?"

I shake my head. "Some girl who lives on the rez. Apparently Butch is nuts about her."

Adrian scoffs. "The poor girl."

We get through the wings just as our break is ending. I tell Joe and Adrian I'll meet them on stage after I use the can.

In the crowded bathroom I meet two locals, and both tell me how much they love the band. Feeling taller, I quickly do my business and head back to the stage.

Just as I sit at my kit, I look over to my right and see Butch bending over a table and talking to some people. Then I see someone pass him two shooters, and he swills both down as soon as he grabs them.

I shake my head. That sonofabitch! I bet he didn't even call that Dakota girl. He's probably been power drinking ever since he left us in the back room.

I hope like hell he keeps it together for the next two sets. This is a great gig for us. If he blows it for the band, I'll never forgive him.

Barney returns to the sound board, and I watch Butch as he sways a little before getting up on stage. Instantly my chest tightens and I feel a rush of anxiety. On our next break, I'm going to confront him and tell him he's an asshole.

We play two songs in a row; both are Southern rock covers that fill the dance floor. We're just starting the third song of the set when a guy on the dance floor accidentally bumps into the stage in front of Butch. I watch as Butch kicks the man hard in the shoulder, sending him skidding on the floor. Both Adrian and Joe look back at me with wide eyes. This isn't good.

People on the dance floor help the man up, then begin to scream at Butch, calling him a bully and a prick. It doesn't take long before Butch sets his bass down on the stage and jumps into the small crowd, throwing fists at everyone he can reach. I hear Joe say, "Oh shit! Here we go again."

The house lights quickly come on. Out of the corner of my eye I see the manager with a face full of anger making his way to the stage. I quickly get up and hurry down the stage steps, hoping to run interference between the manager and Butch. But I'm not fast enough.

In a whirl of fists and fury, Butch's leg connects with the old manager and sends him ass over tea kettle to the floor. As soon as the patrons from the tables see what's going on, they rush to the dance floor to help the bar manager.

By the time I make it to the tangled mob, Butch is going mental. There's a sinister and crazed look on his face and he's so fired up, he's not even looking where his punches and kicks are landing. I make it to him before he gets brought down by the mob. Pushing my way through the dance floor, I'm finally able to grab onto Butch's shirt. "Stop, Butch," I yell. "Enough!"

It's when he glances at me for a brief second that I see something in his eyes I have never noticed before. It's a void, a darkness, and an overwhelming desire to hurt as many people as possible before he is stopped.

A chill runs over me. I let go of his shirt and slowly back away from the growing brawl. Joe and Adrian are still on stage, a safe distance from the violence as they look down on the riot.

I'm not sure how long I've been standing here, helpless and frustrated, when I see police file into the bar, around ten officers. They make their way to the manager, who is sitting down at the bar holding a wad of tissue to his nose. He points to the centre of the stage. The cops then forge into the thicket of the fight, yelling and barking at everyone to get back. Much to my surprise, it works. Soon, the small crowd recedes, leaving only Butch in the middle of the dance floor.

The patrons yell and point at him, shouting *bully* and *asshole*. Butch makes eye contact with the nearest officer, then cracks a smile; it's obvious he's not ready to give up the fight quite yet. He's having too much fun.

After repeated ignored commands from the cops, the taser gun comes out. Butch laughs and yells, "Bring it on."

The prongs are discharged and make instant contact. Butch flops to the floor like a wounded wildebeest. In a flash, four officers land on top of Butch and slap cuffs on him. For the first time since the incident began, I finally exhale.

Soon after, Butch is led out of the bar, kicking and swearing the entire way. By this point, most of the other patrons have filed out.

I spot the manager at the bar. With my tail between my legs, I make my way over to him. I'm just about to speak when he shakes his head at me, then removed the Kleenex from his nose. "Get your gear and get the hell out of my bar. Now!"

"But the other guys and me weren't involved. We would never cause trouble. We just came to play."

He scoffs. "You'll never darken the doorstep of this place again. Get your shit and get the hell out. And if you think you're getting paid, think again. You're lucky I don't sue you."

As the last words leave his lips, two big men walk up and stand beside him. Point taken. There's no way I'm doing damage control now.

Butch fucked us once again, but this time, royally. This was a great gig, and the manager was loving the response we were getting. Now, not only will we never be invited back, but if word of this reaches other venues, all of our future bookings will be at risk.

First thing tomorrow, I'm calling our agent to ask what to do next. Maybe he'll suggest renaming the band. After an initial few minutes of yelling, of course.

I'm so angry and embarrassed by the time I reach the stage; I tear down my kit in half the time it usually takes me. Joe and Adrian don't even have to ask what the manager said. They can tell by my face that it wasn't good. Once we're all loaded out and the van is packed, we pile into the vehicle and head for the hotel.

"Are we leaving in the morning?" Adrian asks.

I shake my head. "No such luck. We have to be out of the hotel tonight. The bar pays for our accommodations. And the manager wants us out now."

24

"Did he pay you any money for the set we did?" Joe says.

I laugh. "Yeah right, Joe. Not bloody likely. And after using almost all our cash to pay for the trip out here, I'd be amazed if we have enough to pay for gas home."

As we pass the front desk on the way to our rooms, the night clerk tells us a police officer dropped off his card and asked that we call him as soon as possible. A hard lump forms in my throat. I tell the guys to go upstairs and pack their things while I call the officer.

Sitting in an armchair in the lobby, I slide out my phone, take a deep breath, and call the cop.

When the officer answers, he sounds somewhat out of breath. They must've had a hell of a time getting Butch into a cell.

As soon as the cop catches his breath, he says we need to come down to the station to give a statement about what happened at the bar. Hoping he'll have compassion and just do a quick phone interview instead, I explain our situation and how we need to get on the road as soon as possible. No such luck, as I expected.

For a moment I wonder what would happen if we just headed out anyway, but never being in trouble with the law before, I know it's best to just comply.

I hurry upstairs and inform the guys, then go to my room and stuff everything into my bag. We then get back into the van and reluctantly head to the police station.

* * *

The bright buzz of florescent lights immediately cause my eyes to hurt. From down a long, white brick hallway comes the sound of frustrated voices. Soon, a female cop appears and asks us our names and why we're here. After we answer her questions, she directs us to a small white room off the hallway. "Wait here for the officer who spoke to you on the phone. He's a little busy taking statements from others who were at the bar."

Joe and Adrian take a seat on the metal chairs while I opt to stand. I'm far too pissed to sit.

It seems like forever before the officer enters the room. He's young, a lot younger than he sounded on the phone—mid twenties, our age. But he looks stressed and fatigued. Poor bastard. I'm sure they weren't expecting to deal with someone as crazed and violent as Butch tonight.

Sliding over a long pad and three pencils, he tells us to write our names, date of birth, address, and our accounting of what we saw unfold at the bar. None of us are writers and none of us are versed in this process, so it takes a good hour for us to finish his request. By the time we're done, all of us are exhausted from the night and ready to head home. The cop tells us that if he has any further questions, he'll reach out.

He follows us out of the room and just before he lets us out, he says, "Oh. I almost forgot. Ray, your friend Butch is going to be calling you shortly. We're allowing him one call."

I shake my head. "First of all, he is definitely not my friend, and secondly, why does he want to talk to me?"

The cop shrugs. "I don't know. He said something about his bass guitar and how it's his livelihood. He said that he needed to make sure you were in charge of it."

"His livelihood?" Joe lets out a laugh. "The guy can't play mediocre on a good day. If that bass is his livelihood, the bugger would starve."

The officer opens the entrance door. We're walking across the lot towards the van when my cell rings. I don't have to look at the screen. I know exactly who it is.

I press the phone to my ear. "What?"

"Hey, Ray. What's going on, man? Did you see how I got jumped at the bar? That was insane."

I sigh. "What do you want, Butch?"

"Oh. It's like that, is it. You don't believe me?"

"I don't give a shit anymore about your excuses. Why did you call me?"

"Fine. We'll talk when I'm out of here and I get back home. In the meantime, I need you to call my cousin Billy and tell him where

I am. Give him my bass, too. He'll probably have to sell it to get my ass out of here."

"Fine. Goodbye, Butch."

"Wait, man. I know you're pissed, but once I explain what happened, you'll understand. Okay, buddy?"

I can't help but laugh. "I already understand, Butch. You were piss drunk, as usual, and then you—"

"Drunk?" he interrupts. "What the hell are you talking about? I never touched a drop. I swear."

"Forget it, Butch. I saw you. Enough with the lies. I will do this one last thing for you. I'll call Billy and give him your bass. Other than that, the ties between you and the band are broken for good. You just blew the best gig we had and we're done. This was your last shot and you blew it. You're out."

There's a long pause. I'm just about to end the call when I hear a sinister voice on the other end. "If you fire me, you will live to regret it, Ray. I am a member of the band as much as any of you. Without me, there is no band. I'll make sure of that."

An eerie feeling runs over me. I've never heard this voice before—not directed at me, anyway. The first thought that enters my mind is, *he's a fucking maniac. He's certifiable.*

I hang up the phone, then reiterate to the guys everything that Butch said to me. Both are stunned. They're well aware that Butch is a bully, and once he sets his mind to torment

someone, he follows through with a
vengeance.

Chapter 3

The ride home is sketchy at best, with a skint amount of gas in the tank and our pockets drained. We pull up to the house on fumes. All of us are completely spent, both emotionally and physically, which is probably a good thing. I'm too tired to be angry, which means that after we unload the van, I'll go straight to bed and sleep like a baby.

Early in the morning, I get up to pee, then make the decision to call Butch's cousin. I quickly explain the situation, then tell Billy that he needs to pick up the bass as soon as possible. Billy sounds irritated, but not at all surprised.

I pour myself a glass of water and wait at the kitchen table for the knock at the door. I hope I can still go back to sleep once I meet Billy.

After an hour of waiting, I'm wide awake and thinking about damage control. My first step will be calling our agent once his office opens. I'm sure he's already heard from the bar manager about everything that happened, so I'm going to have to do some fast talking just to stay on the roster.

I hear Billy's truck pull up, so I get up and meet him at the door with the bass. He looks as tired as me, and just as frustrated. He tells me that this is the last damn time he bails Butch out of shit. "The next time this happens, he's on his own."

We talk for a few minutes, mostly about what a fuck up Butch is, then Billy takes the bass from me and turns to leave. As he walks away, he says over his shoulder that Butch isn't very welcome on rez right now. "He keeps stalking a young girl and her friends."

"Is her name Dakota?"

Billy turns around fully with a look of surprise. "Yeah. Why? Do you know her?"

"No. But Butch was rambling on and on about her. You should tell her to watch her back and be careful. He's not stable."

Billy scoffs. "Tell me about it. The only reason I'm even helping him this time is because I'm worried what he'll do to me and my family if I don't."

Once the door is closed, I decide to head back to bed. Even if I'm too stressed out to sleep, at least I can rest my body before I have to face the day.

* * *

After I've had my first cup of coffee, I take a deep breath and dial up our agent.

As soon as he hears my voice, there's a long pause. I know what's coming—a massive chew-out.

When he finally speaks, he's managed to compose himself. Instead of hollering, he calmly tells me that our band will never be booked again if Butch is involved in any way. I'm quick to agree to his terms. I reassure him that the band has no desire to even speak to Butch again, let alone have him onstage.

Once that issue has been dealt with, we discuss the current state of the music industry in both Saskatchewan and Manitoba, the only two provinces where we play. He says that although a lot of bars are discontinuing bands and hiring DJ's, there are still some places hiring live music, mostly in rural areas. "I'll get back to you as soon as I hear anything regarding gig."

I let out a sigh of relief once the call is over, then share the news with Joe and Adrian. Both are grateful that the agent didn't shit can us.

Joe and I do chores around the house as Adrian calls his bass player friend, George, to arrange a meeting. I'm just thankful Adrian gave him our set lists months ago. At least he'll be familiar with the tunes and it'll save a lot of time in rehearsals. Apparently George is a good bass player. That being said, even if he sucks, he can't be any worse than Butch.

Once all the chores are done and the place looks half-assed again, I head out to the rez to spend some time with Mom.

* * *

A beautiful yellow glow illuminates the snow-covered fields. As much as I'm not a fan of winter, every season is beautiful in Northern Manitoba.

By the time I reach the rez, George has already texted a thank you for the job. At least he's grateful, which means he'll hopefully do his best to impress us. Adrian confirmed that George doesn't drink or do drugs, so that's obviously a huge bonus. We don't want anymore repeat performances of a drunk and disorderly bass player.

The screen door creaks when I swing it open , something my mother has been on me to fix for quite a while. I turn the knob to the main door, hoping it's locked but, again, it isn't.

As soon as I walk in, Mom yells from the kitchen: "Is that you, Ray?"

I shake my head and walk to the kitchen, where Mom is standing over a pot at the stove. "It's me, yes. But it may not have been. I told you, Mom, you need to lock the front door. What if some criminal came in here while you were alone?"

She laughs. "They'd leave this place pretty empty-handed. I don't have much of value."

"It's not your stuff I'm worried about, Mom. It's you."

"Don't worry about me. I've lived here for so long and I know everyone. Plus, I can hear when anyone comes in, thanks to that squeaky screen door you haven't fixed yet."

She's got me there. "Okay. Just promise that you'll start locking the front door when I'm not here."

She glances at me briefly. "Okay. I will try and remember that. So, what are you doing here? Are you just here for your usual few minutes or is there a reason for your visit?"

I sigh. "I know that I don't spend as much time visiting you as I should. I spend every free minute practicing, rehearsing, or dealing with our agent. But I'm here to spend the day and night with you, if that's okay? Maybe we could go through some old albums and watch a movie or something."

She smiles at the thought. "It would be great to spend some time together. But first, I need to bring some canned jars of moose meat to Eileen's."

There's nothing more unappealing to me that going with my mother to visit one of her hen pals. Every time I've accompanied her to see friends in the past, I get stuck for hours as the women gab and gossip.

It's grueling. Still, I'm here unannounced, so I cant really dictate what we're going to do today. I'm at my mother's mercy.

* * *

Eileen is as round as she is tall, but that doesn't stop her from doing anything. It doesn't matter if she has company for an hour or several; the woman doesn't sit down once. Today, sitting at her kitchen table is much the same. Mom and I sip our coffees and ol' Eileen stands on a stool behind us, cleaning out her cupboards. I play a word game on my phone and try to block out the chatter and gossip between the two women.

After another cup of coffee, my mother finally stands. Just when I think we're able to leave, there's a knock at the door. All I can think is, *Please don't let there be another woman coming to visit. My mother will start gabbing again, and any hope of getting out of here will be destroyed.*

Eileen shimmies off the stool and quickly heads to the door. Sure enough, in walks Mabel from down the road, but she's not alone. A young woman who looks to be in her early twenties is right behind her.

As soon as Eileen closes the door behind them, the girl looks up at me, and all of my senses freeze—she's stunning. She looks like a model, standing at about five-eight with a figure that's perfect, slim, and toned.

Eileen introduces the newcomers. "And this is Mabel's niece, who's new to the rez. Her name is Dakota."

My mother says hello and Dakota smiles at me. Her hair is wavy and sits just below her shoulders, framing her perfect face.

"Sit. Sit." Eileen points to the empty chairs at the table.

My mom grabs her coat from the back of the chair. "We were just leaving, actually."

Mabel sighs. "But we just got here."

I scratch my neck. "Um. Yeah, Mom. What's your hurry? It's not like we have any big plans or anything today."

My mother looks at Dakota, then at me. She doesn't say anything, but I can tell by the look on her face that she knows exactly why I want to stay. Then, she puts her coat back where it was on the chair and sits down.

Eileen offers the two women some coffee, then sits with everyone at the table. As the older women talk, I glance up at Dakota and roll my eyes. She giggles and puts her head down, making her all the more appealing.

Just as I'm sipping my new coffee, something occurs to me. Did Eileen say that this girl's name is Dakota? That's not a very common name here on the rez. In fact, the only time I've heard that name lately is when Butch talked about a young woman on rez with that same name. *Oh, please don't be the same girl.*

Down deep, I know the odds are against me. I know this has to be the same young woman. Butch described her as beautiful. Well, this Dakota certainly is that.

Mabel brings up the fact that I'm in a band, then asks what kind of music we play. I can see that Dakota is interested in my answer because her eyes are fixated on me.

I list off some of the songs we play, and Dakota smiles. "Do you play original music as well?"

"Yeah. We're just starting to. We have four or five tunes we've been incorporating into our sets."

"That's great. Do you play around here anywhere?"

"Sometimes we play at the pub in Wakeville, not far from where I live."

"Oh. You don't live on the rez?" She sounds a little disappointed.

Much to my horror, my mother interjects. "No. My son thought he should move away from home so he could become a successful musician. He says there are too many distractions here for him."

Thanks, Mom, for making me sound like a stuck-up asshole.

Dakota nods. "I understand that. I haven't been here for more than a few months and I already notice that it's hard to concentrate. Too many people living too close together, and all of them are pretty noisy."

"Yes! That's exactly it!" I send a pointed look to my mother.

Mabel then asks my mother about canned meat, and the three older ladies start talking among themselves. Dakota leans across the table toward me. "So, where can I come and watch your band?"

"I'm not quite sure when our next gig is. We have an agent working on that as we speak. Sometimes we know where we're playing weeks in advance, but other times it's only a couple days before when we're told."

"Well, you'll have to let me know. I swear, there is nothing to do around here. I've met a few girls since I've been here, but most of them have kids or small siblings that they take care of. Needless to say, I've been spending a lot of time on my own."

I ask her where she's originally from, and she tells me she grew up in Moosejaw, Saskatchewan with her father. "But since he passed away a year ago, it got too expensive to keep living there on my own. I didn't have much choice but to move here and stay with Aunty Mabel. At least, not until I find a job and save a bit of money. Then I'll move off-rez and get my own apartment." She leans even closer, her voice dropping to a whisper. "I can't wait."

I laugh and nod, relating completely to what she's saying.

We just begin talking about things she's done since coming here when Mom pipes up and announces that we should be leaving. "We're going home to watch a movie."

Who cares about the stupid movie, Mom! Can't you see I'm talking to this extremely hot girl? I shoot my mother a quick look, hoping she'll somehow read my mind, but no such luck. She pulls on her coat and walks to the door. Reluctantly, I follow her.

Mom and I walk on the crunchy snow toward home. When we reach the half-way mark, she turns and looks up at me. "What's got you all happy?"

"What do you mean?"

"Well, you've been grinning like a schoolboy since we left Eileen's."

"I have no idea what you're talking about."

She nudges me with her elbow, then chuckles. She knows exactly why I'm grinning. But she also knows that if I'm smitten with a girl, I would never admit it, especially to her. She'd never quit teasing me, and then she'd tell her little group of hens and it would travel around the rez like wildfire. I don't think I want to subject myself to that level of embarrassment.

Just after we reach the house, my cell rings. It's Adrian. He tells me that he and Joe are super excited about George joining the band and there's a tentative plan for a rehearsal tomorrow. "Oh, and I heard Butch got let out on bail. Billy apparently managed to sell the bass quickly and put up the money."

A sick feeling comes over me. After what Butch said to me the last time we spoke on the phone, I don't want to be in the same postal code as that nut bar. All my excitement over meeting Dakota quickly vanishes. The only thing worse than running into Butch while he's pissed over getting kicked out of the band would be if he found out I met his muse, Dakota.

Mom offers me a bowl of moose stew, but I'm too anxious to eat. I wish I was home right now—at least I'd have Adrian and Joe if Psycho Boy showed up drunk. Safety in numbers. Plus, I really don't want any crazy stuff going on while I'm at my mother's. She's lived through more than enough drama while she was with my father and has earned the right to peace in her life.

I sit on the couch while Mom fixes up some hot chocolate. I flip through the channels, looking for something distracting to watch, and eventually land on the old western classic, *High Noon*.

Mom sets the drinks on the coffee table before sitting down close beside me. I can tell she's happy I'm here. Other than get-togethers with her friends, she's alone most of the time ever since I moved out. I feel shitty about that. I love my mom more than anything.

I need to make more time in my life for her. She'd love that. Even if I only had an hour or so during the week, I could take her for a drive to Wakeville and treat her to lunch.

I can't wait until the band starts making money. Ever since I was little, I've dreamt about my mom living in a nice little apartment far away from the reservation. I mean, there's nothing bad about living on the rez, if you're fine with nosy neighbors and everyone in your business. I'd just like to see her have experiences away from here, with new surroundings. Maybe she'd make new friends and have some fun. Here on the rez, nothing changes much. Other than Dakota, there haven't been any new residents in years. People don't flock here—they fight to move away. And yet, even if they do, folks who leave end up coming back within a year, feeling as if they've failed.

By the time the movie ends, I'm starving. I get up and am just walking to the kitchen when there's a hard rap on the door. My first thought is that it's Butch, but then I remember he's still a long way away and couldn't possible have gotten here so quickly.

When I open the door and see Dakota, I'm shocked, and can't help but smile.

I invite her in out of the cold, but she has Mabel in tow and says she can't stay. She reaches out her hand and passes me a small piece of paper. "It's my number. Don't lose it. Text me when you get the details of where you're playing next."

My heart beats fast. "Thanks. I'll be in touch."

She makes to turn away, but then looks back. "You can also get a hold of me to say hi. I'm usually free to talk, since there's not much to do around here, especially in the wintertime."

"That's great. Thanks. I'll reach out, for sure."

I close the door and grin from the inside out. Then I turn around and immediately see my mother smiling. "Let me guess. Was that Mabel and her niece?"

"Stop it, Mom. I don't even want to talk about it with you."

I can still hear her laughing as I step into the kitchen to get myself a bowl of stew.

* * *

Night comes quickly as we watch movies and talk. She asks about Butch, and I tell her everything that happened in Flin Flon. She's horrified about his behaviour and gets into a bad funk until I inform her we already have a new bass player that seems promising. She seems relieved. As much as she hates me living away from home, she really does love the idea of me being a musician. Her father, whom she was extremely close to, was an incredibly skilled guitar and harmonica player. She always said that my love for music came from him.

She has only seen me play a few times, and only on the rez when I was a teen. I remember being in the lodge, playing my heart out, and seeing her clapping and smiling. She was so proud.

My father would have been happy that I became a musician. At least, I think he would have been. From what I've heard from his old buddies, he was a huge fan of playing and watching live music. Sometimes I want to ask Mom about him, but I always stop myself. I don't want to make her remember him and get depressed.

Mom makes us both a sandwich, and after we eat she hugs me and says to shut off the TV when I'm finished watching it. Then, she goes to bed.

After watching a few reruns, I grab a blanket and pillow and head back to the couch.

* * *

A hard *thump* wakes me.

I get up from the couch and look out the window into the dark night. I can't see a thing.

The clock on the wall says 3AM. I lie back on the couch and am just falling back to sleep when a large rock smashes the living room window and lands just feet away from me.

I'm off the couch and at the front door in seconds, my heart thundering as I slide my shoes on. Just as I'm about to open the door, Mom appears. "What in the hell happened?"

"Someone through a rock through the window. I'm going outside to see what's going on."

43

"Be careful. It could be that psycho Butch."

She said exactly what I was thinking. As far as I know, Mom has never had to deal with vandalism while living here. Butch's recent threat to me makes him a likely suspect.

I forgo my jacket and head out the door. In the frigid air, I stand on the front step and look around. When I don't see anyone, I look for footprints in the hard, crunchy snow, but it's too dark to distinguish old prints from new.

When the cold starts to get to me, I head back inside. Mom is sweeping up glass from the broken window. I quickly run into the back room and search until I find an old box and some wide tape.

"Mark my words, Ray." My mother dumps the glass into the garbage. "Butch had something to do with this. He's no good." She heads back to bed.

I make a temporary window patch with the cardboard, then sit down on the couch. All of the tiredness I was feeling before has disappeared. If Butch is responsible for chucking the rock, who knows what else he'll do? I've got to stay awake, at least until the sun comes up. Just in case.

Through the night, I contemplate having my mother stay at my place with Joe and Adrian, just until I make sure that she'll be safe alone. But then I remember how crazy she used to get when we practiced in the back room. She never could handle the noise. Besides, she'd drive my roommates crazy with her clean freak ways.

The only other thing I can do to ensure her safety is to talk with the chief. He always has a way of defusing disputes.

* * *

Mom gets up at 7AM and heads into the kitchen to make a pot of coffee.

I follow her, yawning. "I guess we'd better figure out how to get your window fixed."

"Why? They'll just break it again. Don't do anything until we figure out who did it."

"How will we find that out? It's not like they'll come knocking on the door and take responsibility."

Mom giggles. "Obviously you don't know the power of gossip. As soon as I put out the news about what happened, it will spread through the community in a matter of minutes. Someone will have seen something. Mark my words."

"Okay. Fine. We can wait a bit to see if we hear anything, but in the meantime, I want to stay here to make sure you're safe."

"No. That's not necessary. I will be fine. Besides, you should go home and practice with your new bass player. The band needs to be ready when the agent calls with work."

She's right, of course. But I still don't feel confident about leaving her here in the house

45

alone, especially at night, with a broken window. But I can tell she's made her mind up about the way things should be, and once that happens, it might as well be set in stone.

Over coffee, we discuss a safety plan in case something bad does happen while I'm not here. I finally get her to agree to keep her phone by her bed, and if she hears anything alarming, she will call me immediately.

Chapter 4

On the drive home, my head is racked with worry about my mom's safety. If I can't sleep after rehearsal tonight, I'll drive back to the rez and park across the street from her house and watch who comes and goes.

It's after 10AM when I walk through the door. Adrian and Joe are at the kitchen table having breakfast. Before heading to my room to get changed, I tell them about what happened at Mom's. They immediately look at each other, and Joe says, "I don't think it's a mystery who's responsible."

Adrian asks if we saw anyone running away after the window was broken.

I shake my head. "Not a soul. And the ground was firm with frozen snow, so no obvious prints were visible."

"This morning, I heard Butch is back on the rez. That's what my aunty told me."

I nod. "I figured as much. Did she say when he got back?"

"No. She just said the overall feeling about him returning isn't good."

It isn't going to help to mull over Butch. Not until I know for sure it was him. So I change the subject. "Tell me about George. Have either of you heard him play before?"

"I have," Adrian says. "He's really good. Miles better than Butch ever was."

"Is he coming over today to rehearse?"

"Yeah. He has to drive his mother into town for groceries. After that, he'll come by."

* * *

The shower is running and I'm just about to slip out of my jeans when my cell rings. I don't recognize the number on the screen. "Hello?"

"I heard what happened at your mom's place. Is everyone okay?" It's an unfamiliar female voice.

"Fine. Thanks. Who is this?"

She giggles. "It's Dakota."

"Oh. Wow. Cool. Um, I didn't think you had my number."

"I didn't, but it didn't take me long to find it once I asked around. Not much is private on the rez."

"Tell me about it."

"Do you mind that I have your phone number?"

"No. Not at all. I'm glad you called."

Dakota asks me the details about what happened at Mom's. I close the toilet seat and sit down while I recount the rock through the window and my suspicions over who might be responsible.

48

"Butch is crazy out of his mind," she says. "Ever since I moved on rez, the guy has been pretty much stalking me. I've tried talking to him about it, but he just denies ever following me. It's unnerving and creepy. I wish he'd just leave me alone."

"I'm sorry that you're going through that. Butch has never paid much attention to what's right or wrong. Mostly. He prefers to conduct his life doing wrong. But if you're worried about him, you should really talk to the chief."

"I was thinking of doing that. I just don't want to bring a lot of attention to the situation. I guess I thought it may piss Butch off and cause him to act even weirder around me."

"Trust me. The chief has a lot of pull. He won't put up with anyone intimidating anyone else. He puts an end to bad behaviour really quickly."

"Maybe you're right." Dakota gets quiet for a moment, then tells me that if she catches Butch following her again, she'll go and see the chief. "So, anyway—what are you doing with the rest of your day?"

"I have rehearsal. Probably be at it for most of the day."

"Well, if you're bored later and want to talk, just text me."

I happily agree, then end the call with the biggest smile.

Once I'm showered and dressed, I head to the front room and wait with the guys until George shows up. He's shorter than the rest of us, with long hair tied in the back. He looks clean and has a pleasant disposition as he shakes our hands and thanks us for the opportunity to play in the band.

Eager to hear him play, the four of us go to the back room and start jamming a couple of easy covers. At the end of the songs, Joe looks back at me and grins. I know exactly what he's thinking. George is a good player—better than Butch. I love the way he plays with me to make a solid rhythm section.

We spend the next few hours going over some more covers and a few originals. George hits every note and doesn't mess up once. By the end of rehearsal, we're all hungry and decide to order a pizza and sit in the living room and chat.

Adrian pats George on the shoulder and tells him how awesome he was. Joe and I both agree and thank him for saving our butts. Without him being available, not to mention as an accomplished player, we'd have no hope of keeping the band together. Now that we have George, I can call the agent in the morning and reassure him that we're all set to go. Maybe after we play a few gigs without incident, our reputation will start to repair.

When we've finished our food, Adrian asks George if he's heard anything about my mother's house being vandalized.

"No. I mean, there are the usual shit disturbers out late at night. Most are preteens. But as destructive as they can be—spray painting buildings and kicking over trash—I've never heard of any intentionally breaking windows. Most of the broken windows are usually caused by people fighting in their homes, usually when alcohol is involved."

"So it probably was Butch, then," Adrian says. "It makes sense. He's the only one with an ax to grind."

George nods. "He's trouble, in every sense of the word. I wish he'd move away and stay gone. Seems like when something really bad happens, his name is somehow connected. I just hope that he doesn't cause trouble for me or my family. You know, when he finds out about me taking his place in the band."

I nod. "You may want to distance yourself from your family for a while, at least until Butch gets used to the idea of you being our new bass player. That way, if you're not on the rez, he'll have no reason to target your house there."

"I don't have the money to rent my own place. That's the only reason I live on the rez."

"What if you moved in here with us for a while?" Joe suggests. "If you stay at your parents house after joining the band and something happens, I think we'd feel pretty responsible."

George is taken aback. "Really? Are you sure? I mean, I don't make a lot of cash working for my uncle's natural medicines company, but I'm sure when we start doing gigs, I can chip in my share of the rent."

"Don't worry about that now," Adrian adds. "As long as you're off the rez, you and your parents will be a lot safer."

"How many bedrooms in this house? Is there room for me?"

I shrug. "That's a bit of an issue, but if you don't mind sleeping on the hide-a-bed, you can stay in the rehearsal room. There's a big empty closet in there where you can put your stuff."

George thanks us repeatedly, then heads for the door. "I'll stay at home tonight so I can tell my family and pack a suitcase. I'll be back tomorrow."

We say goodbye, then the three of us head to our rooms. Once in bed, I slide my phone out of my pocket and text Dakota.

Immediately she messages me back, asking how rehearsal went. I tell her how awesome George played and how I can't wait to get on the road and play some live shows.

She seems genuinely excited that we were able to fill Butch's position with an even better bass player. I like that about her. Most of the girls I've been around have little or no interest in the band. Mostly, they listen to country or pop songs they find on YouTube. Dakota's positive energy about live music makes me want to know her better. For that reason, and also because she's hot as hell.

For a moment, I imagine what it would be like to have her come over and visit. I cringe thinking about Adrian and his impromptu farting, and how he tries to name each one. Then there's Joe. Although he doesn't do anything outwardly vile, Joe tends to ramble on for hours about the most mundane subjects. On the van ride back from Flin Flon, he spent the entire time talking about his conspiracy theories and almost drove Adrian and I nuts. That being said, he is my best friend, or the closest thing I have to one.

"Ray," Dakota says, "are you still there? Or did you fall asleep?"

"Sorry. I spaced out for a minute there."

"How often do you come to the rez?"

"Not very. Much to my mother's regret. I mean, if there's a significant function or meeting, I'll go. Yesterday I was at the lodge for the announcement of the vision quest a few men from our village will be embarking on. And I try and go back to see my mom when I can."

"If I had a place off-rez, I'd never come back. I can't stand living so close to everyone." She laughs. "If you sneeze, the neighbor says bless you."

"I know what you mean. I couldn't handle it. I felt claustrophobic there and everyone knows everyone else's business. I don't know why anyone in our age group chooses to live on rez. Maybe when I'm old I'll move back, be amongst my relatives and the people I grew up with, but not now. I've got too much living to do."

"I feel the same way. The first chance I have to work in a town or city, my bags are packed."

She asks about my parents. My mom is an easy subject, but my father, not so much. When I tell her that he left my mom years ago, then got sick and died, she almost sounds like she's tearing up. "That's terrible."

"It is what it is. At least he wasn't abusive or anything. I think he just wanted to move away and experience life. Knowing my mother, who has never seen a reason to live anywhere else, she probably didn't want to go with him, so he just opened the door, walked out, and never looked back."

"But what about you? You were his son. Don't you begrudge him for being so selfish?"

"Yes and no. It would've been nice to have a father, especially when I was going through my teens. I would've loved for him to take me fishing and hunting and to teach me about our traditions. But on the other hand, I get why he moved away. Maybe he felt the same way as I do. Maybe he knew there was no future for him around here."

"That's very good of you to try and see his side of things. How does your mother feel about him leaving?"

"Hurt, mostly. Even though it's been years since he left, she still keeps whatever clothes he left behind in the closet. Once I asked if I could use one of his sweaters and she wouldn't let me. In some ways, I think she always thought he might come back."

"And how did you hear about him being sick?"

"We didn't hear he was sick until after he passed. We got a call from a young guy that said he was his son. He told us that my father had been living in Winnipeg and had taken up with a Cree woman there. Dad was diagnosed with cancer but managed to live with it for years. Before he died, he told his young son about my mom and me and said he should call us."

"I'm so sorry, Ray. And did you and his teenage son keep in touch?"

"I wanted to, but no. My mom was so betrayed by him hooking up with another woman and starting a family while we were here waiting for him. I didn't want to hurt her by having contact with his new son and wife."

"I feel so badly for you, and of course your mom, too. But it would've been nice if you and his young son stayed connected. I think it would've been good for both of you."

"Yeah. I think about him sometimes. Maybe one day we'll meet in person. There's still lots of time."

"Never as much as we think."

"So, what about you? Why are you living on the rez with your aunty? Where were you before?"

"I was living up in York Factory with my sister and her family. She's a lot older, and after my mom died, she practically raised me."

"Your mother passed? I am sorry, Dakota."

"Don't be. I was only five, and most of what I remember is that she was abusive. I never knew who my father was. We had our suspicions, but nothing was ever proven."

"So you grew up in York Factory? Why did you decide to leave?"

"Let's just say that my sister's husband changed one day. Or should I say, one night. He came into my room after partying all night and tried to take advantage of me. I yelled for my sister, and when she came into the room and saw him lying on top of me, trying to take my clothes off, she got mad at me. Suggested that I'd been trying to seduce him for a long time. I couldn't believe it. Anyways, I called my aunty, and the rest is history. For now, anyway."

"That sucks. Are you angry with your sister?"

"If I think about it too much. I think what pisses me off most is that I was her live-in babysitter to her three kids. I can't imagine what she's doing for a nanny now. Both she and my stupid brother in-law chopped and sold firewood. They're definitely in a bad situation now, since only one can work. Oh well. I bet my sister is second guessing her decision now."

"I'm sorry she didn't side with you and kick his ass out."

She laughs. "I'm sure she is too!"

I hear someone call her name. "Is that your aunt?"

"Yeah. I should probably go, but it was nice talking to you. I'll call you another time, when I don't have an audience."

After the call ends, I lie on the bed and look up at the ceiling. Dakota seems so level-headed and cool. I'd love to get to know her better.

Still, I can't help but feel that the closer I get to her, the more danger I'll create for myself. Maybe for my mother, too.

* * *

A constant pour of water spills over the eaves and punches a large hole in the crunchy ice below. Finally, the weather is changing, and the snow is starting to melt.

It's been ten days of George living here, and every free moment we've spent rehearsing. I've been driving past Mom's house every couple of nights and calling her at least once a day. So far, the vandalism has stopped. As for Butch, I've not seen hide nor hair of him, though Adrian says that he's been hanging around the rez with his cousin, Billy.

As for Dakota, we have been touching base every evening, usually after I've showered and climbed into bed. She's amazing—the perfect girl.

After a week of not hearing from our agent, he finally called yesterday. He's booked us into a hotel with a small pub in it. It's located in North Battleford Saskatchewan, far enough away that Butch wouldn't waste his energy coming by. We've never played the venue before—we've got to do well so we're asked back. We leave tomorrow morning, set up in the evening, then play the next night.

I'm just packing my suitcase when there's a rap on my bedroom door. I yell, "Enter," and Joe walks in.

"Hey, man. Are you packing for the gig?"

"No. I just thought I'd time myself on how long it takes to pack a suitcase in case there's a fire."

"Funny."

"What's up?"

"I just wanted to speak to you alone for a minute."

"Okay. What about?"

"The band. I've been researching a lot of sites where they post ads for musicians for hire."

Perplexed, I remind him that we already have a band. A good one, thanks to George.

Joe shakes his head. "No, you don't get it. Some of the musicians looking to form new bands are pro-players. They list their creds and a few of them have played A-rooms in Vancouver and Toronto. They've made a name for themselves."

"So, who cares? We can make a name for our band, too."

"Ray. Think about it, man. Why would we waste our time drudging away at these half-assed gigs when we could just join an already established band? Seriously. Besides, who's to say that our band will ever take off. More often than not, guys just get old on the road, and nothing good ever happens for them. Do you want that to be us?"

I stop packing and sit down on the corner of the bed. "Dude. You're not making a whole lot of sense to me. We've practiced since we were kids to become the best players we could. And our efforts paid off."

"Exactly. That's what I'm saying, Ray. Why waste any more time? I think we should send in a tape of us both playing separately. I think a lot of musicians will see that we're capable of playing venues."

I shake my head. "What about Adrian and George? They'd never have a chance of forming a new band without us. There aren't enough good players around here. Plus, Adrian is a follower, not a leader. He'd never be able to deal with booking agents and gigs. Not to mention he has zero organizational skills, something you kind of need when you're running a band."

Joe sighs. "I know. I know. But look at it this way. We can still play gigs with both

George and Adrian. All I'm suggesting is that while we're working, we also put our names out there, too. And if Adrian and George want to follow suit and do the same thing, great."

"I don't know, man. It kind of sounds like you're giving up on what we worked so hard to build."

"No way. Just the opposite. I want to play all the time, every night if possible. I'm just tired of playing the green run. I want to play on a pro stage with pro players who draw in big audiences. What's wrong with that?"

I tell Joe that I'll think about it, mostly just to get him out of my room. He chatters a lot. He's always been the same. Ever since we were kids, he's always come up with cockamamie ideas, ones that usually never blossomed into anything.

* * *

John Prine blasts through the speakers, George's musical choice. I've never really listened to Prine before, but everything I've heard him do so far has been amazing. He's such a great songwriter and guitar player. To me, he sounds like Country-Folk, with a hint of rock and roll.

The drive to North Battleford Saskatchewan takes about nine hours, and we're already seven hours in. It took a bit longer than expected to get out of the house, as Adrian had to stop at the rez to borrow gas money off his family. It's the downside of being a musician; when gigs dry up for a while, you end up tapping into every bit of savings you have.

Which, in my case, wasn't much. I had saved a bit of money a couple months ago, working as a casual labourer for a friend of the chief's who lives off the rez. The guy has a warehouse filled with broken antiques— old couches, ladders, signs— and my job was to repair them. It was a pretty easy job, considering the guy wasn't super picky or riding my back every two seconds. I'd told him I needed some time off to get the band off of the ground. He was really cool about it and told me I always have a job to come back to if I want it.

George points out the window. "Hey, look at the big horn sheep."

Joe laughs. "Haven't you ever left the rez before?"

George shakes his head. "No. Never. And the closest thing to a round sheep I've ever seen is your mother."

The rest of us laugh. He fits in just fine.

* * *

It's just after dinner time when we pull into North Battleford. It's a clean city, with a mixture of old and new. It's no surprise when we pull up to the Wagoneer Inn and it's on the older side of the street. Musicians usually rank pretty low on the social scale, and so do the gigs we play at and the accommodations we stay in. That is, unless you're an A-room act, which we clearly are not.

We all pile out of the van, take a couple minutes to stretch, then go inside to find out where we can unload our gear.

Even though the bar is aged and a bit raggedy, the stage is a nice size and the ceilings are high. There's nothing worse than playing on a stage that could double as a shoe box.

After setting up my kit, I tell the guys that I'm going upstairs to have a shower and relax. Really, I just want to be alone so I can call Dakota. It's strange, but I don't care if we're just talking about normal life or mundane things. I'm always excited to talk to her—obviously, considering how long we stay on the phone for. Sometimes I'll call her after dinner and we'll talk until the wee hours of the morning. I think she's the first girl I've ever done that with. Speaking with her is effortless and real. I love it.

I'm just getting out of the shower and preparing to lie on my bed and call her when there's a rap on the door. I open the door to Adrian, holding a plastic container. He holds it out. "Here you go. My aunt packed us all some food and snacks."

Grateful, I take the container and thank him.

When I return to the bed and lift up the lid, I see a package of sealed candied salmon, beef jerky and some home-made pastries. The smell is amazing. I wasn't even hungry until now. I guess I was waiting to eat until after we played our first set and the bar lets us have a tab. But now, as I look down at the goodies, my stomach starts to rumble. I quickly unwrap two Nanaimo bar squares, then call Dakota.

Thankfully she answers, and not one of her family members. Like her aunt, who most likely would give me a hard time, asking where I am and what I'm doing and—worse of all—why I want to talk to Dakota. There are some very nosy women on the rez, many Chatty Cathy's who have to know everything, especially when it involves one of their family members.

"How was the drive?" Dakota asks.

"Pretty uneventful." I tell her about the big sheep, and George's joke about Joe's mother bearing a likeness to the creature. Dakota laughs, but I detect a little stress in her voice. "Is there something wrong?"

She takes a few moments to answer. "Butch was asking around. Wondering where you guys are gigging at right now."

"That's weird...and somewhat concerning. Did he find out?"

"I don't think so. I sure didn't say anything to anyone. But you may want to ask the band if they mentioned going to North Battleford. It's probably best that you're prepared in case that psycho makes an appearance."

I take a deep breath, then slowly exhale to shake off my concern. "You know what? I'm not worried. There's no way Butch is going to have his shit together enough to travel over nine hours just to give us a hard time. Plus, he's notoriously broke. Gas is expensive, and something tells me he's used up all his favors on the rez. Even his cousin said he's tired of Butch's antics, so I don't think he'll be offering Butch a ride."

"Okay. If you're sure. I just thought I should let you know, just in case."

"Thanks for caring. You know, you should come with us on one of our road trips. I could room with Joe so you can have your own room." As soon as the words leave my mouth, I feel vulnerable and stupid. I haven't known her very long, even though we've talked a lot on the phone. My offer is a bit presumptuous.

After a few awkward moments of silence, she says, "Really? You want me to come with you? I'd be so happy to get out of here and come to one of your gigs."

Relieved, I let out a laugh. "I'm not so sure if your aunty will feel the same way. About you taking off with me."

"Don't worry about that. When the time comes, I'll figure something out."

"This is great. Now I have something to look forward to."

"When you come back, are you going to attend the powwow at the lodge?"

"When is it?"

"This upcoming weekend."

I'm surprised my mother hasn't said anything about it. She was probably waiting until there was only couple of days before the event to mention it. That way I couldn't come up with an excuse not to go. "Yeah. Of course I'll be there."

"Great. Just keep in mind that Butch will most likely show up."

"I can't worry about that, Dakota. I've been doing some thinking, and although I don't want to get into an altercation with the crazy bastard, I can't live in fear of him forever, either."

Dakota tells me that she has to go, but that she'll text me soon. Before she hangs up, she cautions me to be careful, and to keep an eye out for Butch at the gig, just in case.

* * *

I'm just dozing off when Joe decides to grace me with his presence. I stand at the door in my underwear as he asks if I'd given any thought to what we were discussing back home.

"Actually, Joe, I'm exhausted from the drive. I'm not thinking about anything but sleeping."

Just as I'm closing the door, he adds, "I've already written to a couple of the more well-known musicians on the rock site. I put your name and credentials up there, too."

I yank the door open again. "You what? Why the hell did you do that? I told you that I'd think about it. What if Adrian or George happen to see your post? Don't you think they'd be a little confused, or feel betrayed?"

"Sorry, man. I thought you'd be grateful."

"Grateful? That's bullshit, Joe. You are trying to push me into something that I haven't had time to consider. The reason you included me is because you were too chicken shit to put your name out there alone."

"That's not true. I was looking out for your best interest, as well as my own."

"Whatever. I'm going back to bed." I close the door hard.

Once alone, I lie on my bed and stew about the lack of respect Joe showed me by going behind my back. How could he have thought I'd be okay with him answering an ad with my creds? What a complete shit he is.

On top of my anger is shock. I sort through my memories of him—other than the odd argument about music arrangements, we've always gotten along great. He's never shown me any kind of disrespect. Until now.

It takes hours to shake off the frustration enough to sleep. In what seems like seconds, orange light floods the room and wakes me. When I look at the clock, I see that it's 6AM, which means I've only had two hours of sleep—*thanks a lot, Joe.*

I've never been one to fall back to sleep once I'm awake. So, I decide to get up and occupy myself until the guys get up.

* * *

After grabbing a coffee to-go at an early morning café, I walk around the sleeping streets, checking out store fronts. Once I'm done, I wander back to the café, find a seat, and slide my phone out of my pocket. Thankfully there's Wi-Fi in the small cafeteria, and I can check my emails. Most are junk, but there are a couple from the agent. I read through the information on two possible gigs, both way up North in small towns I've never heard of before. How depressing.

On a whim, I go to the Rock site where Joe posted our bios. I scroll through the long list of posts written by musicians all over Canada. Some ask for tips on where to eat while playing gigs on the road, others post about new gear and ask for opinions on quality. Finally, I get to the post about musicians wanted: a guitar player and a drummer. Apparently an Ontario A-list band—one who's opened for or played with heavy hitters in the industry—is searching for pro players to fill some across-Canada dates. I scroll past at least fifty replies, all from players vying for the job. Finally, I find Joe's comment.

"Two pro players from Manitoba. Versatile styles with unmatchable talent. Drummer and guitar player are ready to roll."

What a complete idiot. He made us sound like icons. Is he nuts? I mean, we're good, but we're not great. At least, I don't think we are.

I remember overhearing something a village elder told some young boys on the rez. "Always treat others as if they were family, and don't let your mouth write a cheque that your ass can't cash." It made perfect sense to me. Though, I think Butch may have missed the meaning of the words all together.

I ask the waitress for another coffee, and just as she's carrying the pot over, Adrian walks into the café. I nod when I see him, and he joins me at my table. He's dishevelled and half awake.

"What's going on, Ray?" he says, before asking the waitress for a coffee.

"You're looking at it. I was up before the birds, so I thought I'd take a cruise around the town, then sit for a bit. Why are you up so early? Did you wet the bed?"

Adrian smirks. "Yeah. That's it."

The waitress returns with a fresh cup of coffee and sets it in front of Adrian. She then asks if we want to order off the breakfast menu. Both of us politely decline.

Once the waitress leaves, Adrian shoots me a grin. "Do you think she'd let us do dishes for a plate of bacon and eggs?"

"It's mind over matter, Adrian. If you tell yourself you're not hungry, you can make it quite a while without food. Anyway, don't you have food left that your family gave you? You must have some goodies still."

He shrugs. "Maybe a bit, but I'm like a squirrel. I like to stow away grub for later." Then, he starts to talk about the band, and asks if I've heard about any upcoming gigs. His eyes are hopeful as he waits for my reply.

"Nothing great. I'm sure in the next few days I'll get another call from the agent, telling me what else is available."

He nods. "Can you ask if he can find some better paying clubs to play at? I can't afford to pay my bills with what we're making."

I chuckle. "I thought you were like a squirrel. Can't you just stow away each dime you make?"

"Not when you visit a house full of family members. Every time I go home after being on the road, they're at me to loan them cash. They're relentless."

The door opens again, and I see George enter the café. He spots us right away and sits down. He motions to the waitress, points at our coffees, then turns to us with a smile. "What did I miss?"

"Adrian was just telling me the drawbacks of having a big family."

"Yeah, well, that's pretty much the same for everyone. I can't wait until our gigs pick up and I can afford to rent my own pad. Not that I begrudge living with you guys." He winks.

Adrian snorts. "I do. I begrudge living with all of you. One of you snores, the other walks around the house late at night, and a third—*Ray*—listens to music too loudly in the early morning."

As we sit and chat, I feel increasingly bad for Adrian and George. They are completely oblivious to Joe cutting them out of the search for a better gig. I've always operated by a code of loyalty regarding the band. We're supposed to be a brethren. In it for the long haul, together. We don't just abandon each other because things get tight. Going through the hard times makes us stronger as a group.

As soon as I can get Joe alone, I'm telling him to take my name off that page. If he still wants to keep searching and hoping for a better set up, that's fine. But not me. As much as I would love the opportunity to play great venues, stay at swanky hotels, and actually play to a big crowd, I'd feel like a shit-heal if I walked out on Adrian and George. They want our band to succeed as bad as I do. So, sink or swim, I'm in it for the long haul.

Chapter 5

With an hour left until we play, the four of us meet in the bar for a quick sound check. There are already a couple of tables of people waiting for the music.

After we go back upstairs and get ready, I quickly call Dakota in hopes that we can talk before starting the night. No such luck. Instead, her aunt answers and tells me that Dakota is out, then proceeds to ask a ton of questions—Why have I been calling Dakota so much? Am I'm looking to make her my girlfriend? And, the worse question of all—am I trying to take Dakota away from her?

Thankfully, Adrian raps on my door and interrupts the call. I tell her that I have to get going, then ask her to tell Dakota that I called. She won't, of course, but it's the only thing I can think of to say before hanging up.

Adrian and I are walking downstairs to the bar when Joe appears at the bottom. "You guys are never going to guess who's standing at the bar."

My chest tightens and I stop walking. Oh, no. *Don't let it be Butch.*

Joe sees my apprehension. "Don't worry, Ray. It's not Butch. I can see on your face that you're worried."

I laugh sarcastically. "I never thought it would be Butch, and if it was, so what? I was just a bit surprised that you would recognize someone in the bar." My chest relaxes, and I draw in a deep breath.

When we walk in the bar, I can see Marty, a guy we went to school with, sitting on a stool. Adrian and I give a quick wave and continue to the stage. Joe stays behind to chat, then soon joins us.

We start the night off with CCR and a few songs by Canned Heat. So far, what little crowd there is seems really into it. When we play a Journey song, two of the three full tables get up to slow dance.

On our first break the manager, a portly woman about fifty, tells us how much she likes the band, right before she asks if we can turn it down—a common request when playing small pubs. The four of us join Marty and talk about what he's been up to lately. We find out he's in North Battleford on a construction job.

Just before our break ends I head to the john, where it's quiet, and dial Dakota. There's no answer. I thought she would have been home by now. I hope everything is all right.

Once we're back on stage, Joe decides to forgo our set list and take requests, which always gets the crowd more into it. Though,

I never expected to be playing a whole set of Country music. Still, if it makes the patrons happy, they stay longer and order more beer, and that makes the bar happy. So, we do our best to accommodate every song request they holler out to us.

* * *

The only thing worse than the creaking pipes is the water pressure. I turn on the taps in the shower and hold my face under the pitiful trickle. It seems as though every small venue we play at on the green run has the same things in common: drafty one-pane windows, noisy pipes, and the weakest water pressure possible.

After I'm dried and into a fresh t-shirt and pair of shorts, I grab my phone. It's 1AM, but last night Dakota said she'd be waiting by the phone and would pick up after the first ring so her aunt wouldn't wake up. I lie back on the pillow, get comfortable, then dial her number.

Her phone rings once, then twice. The last thing I want is to wake up her pushy aunt. I wait for one more ring, then hang up.

That's the second time today Dakota didn't answer. I wish I could call her cell phone, but a while ago she told me it was restricted to local calls only. Confused and a little concerned, I scroll through my phone and check for any missed calls. There aren't any. Not sure what to do next, I turn on the crappy little TV to distract myself.

I'm flipping aimlessly through the limited channels when there's a rap on my door. I shake my head, knowing exactly who it is. Joe. And I bet anything he's come to needle me again about soliciting our names for other bands.

I fling open the door, fully prepared to say I'm in no mood to discuss anything right now, but the words die on my lips. There, in the doorway, is Dakota.

I try to speak, but nothing comes out. She giggles, blinking coyly up at me. "Surprised to see me?"

I'm finally able to get words out. "Wow, Dakota—what are you doing here? I just tried to call you at your aunt's."

"Well, I'm not there."

"I can see that. How did you get here?"

"Maybe you should invite me in and I'll tell you."

I grin. "Yeah. Of course. Come in."

As she walks inside and takes a seat in the small room's singular chair, I reach down and quickly gather up the sweaty stage clothes that I'd thrown on the floor. After depositing them into a drawer, I sit on the corner of the bed, across from her. "I can't believe you're here." My pulse speeds up as excitement runs through me.

She seems aware of my shock. "Is it okay that I'm here? I mean, you said you'd be okay with me coming to one of your gigs."

"And I completely am. It's just...I never dreamt you'd show up to surprise me. I'm blown away. How did you get here?"

"I was at one of my cousin's place today. She had friends visiting from here. They were heading this way, so I caught a ride this morning."

"Well, I'm glad you did. It's a long way to come, though. You must be tired."

"I am. I'm not sure if it's because I was in the car since this morning, or because I was scared you might not be happy when I got here."

"You're kidding, right?"

She shrugs. "Well, I did take a big chance. What if I showed up and you had someone in your room with you? That would've been awkward. Not to mention I would've had to sleep in the lobby or some place."

I shake my head. "I'm nothing like that. The last thing I want is a groupie in my room. It's just not my thing." I check the time. "The only problem is that the front desk is closed now, so I can't charge your room to the band account."

She yawns, then unzips her hoodie. "Would it be okay if I shared a bed with you?" She grins. "I promise to stay on my own side."

"That depends. Do you snore?"

"Horribly. That's the real reason I'm here. I got kicked off the rez for disturbing the peace."

"Nice try."

Knowing that she's tired, I turn the TV off, then lie down on my own side. I keep perfectly still; I don't want to do anything she could perceive as getting fresh.

She thanks me for not being weirded out by her impromptu appearance, then slowly drifts off.

In the darkness of the room, with only the buzzing of the neon sign outside breaking the quiet, I smile. I can't believe that this stunning creature is actually lying next to me.

Then, anxiety creeps into my mind. What if, after spending time with me, she's sees what a bore I am? I mean, I've definitely been around a lot of women and know how they act, but Dakota is different. She breaks all the norms I'm used to. She's independent, funny, sharp....and she's the most beautiful woman I think I've ever seen.

My mind flashes to Butch. How he stalks Dakota. If he could see us now, lying together in bed, he'd probably bust something. Probably me.

Dakota turns onto her back, and the sweet floral smell of her hair wafts toward me. I picture rolling over and wrapping my arm around her. But I wouldn't, not right now. The last thing I want to do is to make her feel unsafe.

* * *

I wake to the bright light of the sun lancing my eyelids. I slowly open them and look down at my chest, where Dakota's head is softly resting.

I feel the corners of my mouth turn upward and wonder if she intentionally snuggled with me or she'd done it while she was sleeping. Staying very still so as not to wake her, I revel in the moment.

Thankfully I can sign for food now that we played and the bar owes us money. If Dakota had shown up yesterday morning, I would've been horrified and embarrassed at not being able to cover her breakfast.

After about a half hour, Dakota stirs and opens her eyes. I quickly close mine, in case she's embarrassed that her head is on my chest. She briefly lifts her head, then lays it back down again.

Inside, I'm beaming. I can't believe it—she's completely comfortable snuggling up to me. I could lie here with her all day, but unfortunately the urge to pee is growing, and eventually I open my eyes, fake yawn, then tap her gently on the shoulder. She looks up at me with a smile. "I'm sorry if I crowded you. I got cold last night."

"That's okay. Although, your enormously sized head was so heavy that it did cut off circulation to my arm. It's completely numb. I just hope I can still play drums tonight."

She looks at me intently. "Are you serious?"

I shake my head and laugh. "Of course not."

* * *

The small diner is packed with locals taking advantage of the breakfast specials. I would suggest that we go to another restaurant, but this place is owned by the hotel and bar that hired us, so we have signing privileges here.

We only wait ten minutes before a group of blue-collar workers in coveralls vacate their table, and after a quick wipe down, the waitress waves us over. We both order the special, which is two eggs, two pieces of toast, and two big sausages.

The café is rumbling with talk and laughter, making it near impossible for Dakota and me to hear one another, so we stay quiet and wait for our food. I slowly scan the busy room and notice that two thirds of the patrons seem to be glaring at us.

Dakota notices the same thing; when our eyes meet, she grins and shrugs her shoulders.

I'm uncomfortable, and I know that Dakota is too. I only wish I could afford to take her some place else. Regardless, I lean across the table and mouth, "Do you want to leave?"

She shakes her head.

After ten minutes, the waitress sets our breakfast in front of us. I'm just about to ask for ketchup when out of my peripheral vision I see the door open and Adrian and George walk in.

Oh great. Just when I thought things couldn't possibly get more uncomfortable.

It doesn't take long before the boys spot us and make their way through the busy café toward our table. Without asking, they sit on either side of us and introduce themselves to Dakota.

Adian looks around the room, then chuckles. "What the hell, man. Why is everyone staring at us?"

"Probably because of how good-looking Dakota is," I say.

"Yeah, well it sure wouldn't be because of your good looks."

A few more tables filter out as the waitress takes our uninvited guests' order. Thankfully, the noise has now died down, and we can hear each other.

"What made you come up to North Battleford, Dakota?" George asks.

"I thought I'd check out your band. Plus, I wanted to get off the rez for a while."

George is just about to say something else when he notices a couple of older men glaring at us from a nearby table. "Whatcha lookin' at, old-timers? Never seen a table full of Indians before?"

I try and shut him up, but I can tell by the look on his face and how stiff his body is that he's going to say what's on his mind.

"What the hell, George?" Adrian hisses. "Don't cause a scene, man. Our boss owns this place."

I glance at Dakota's plate. She has a long way to go before she's finished her breakfast and we can get out of here.

George keeps his eyes on the older men. "I'm not trying to cause a problem. I'm just not sure why they're staring at us. We have a right to come in here and eat, the same as they do."

"Let it be, George," I urge.

"I'll let it be when they quit gawkin' at us."

I look over at the old codgers, hoping they'll divert their attention away from us, but they don't.

"Do you think we're a bunch of savages? Is that the problem?" George continues.

Adrian looks anxious. "Stop. Please."

George smiles at the men. "Maybe us uneducated, lazy, drunk Indians should've stayed on the rez and ate our Bannock and pemmican."

The waitress hears George raise his voice and comes over to the table. "I don't know what the problem is, but you can't be doing this in here. Workers come in to eat before work. If those two guys are bothering you, maybe it would be best if you just left and came back later."

I stand. "Good idea."

Dakota places her napkin on her food and gets to her feet as well. "I think you're right. We can always come back after."

George scoffs. "Yeah, right. Why would we do that when we're not the ones causing the problem? Why don't you ask them to leave?"

The waitress puts her hands on her hips. "Am I going to have to call the owner?"

"Please don't do that," Adrian pipes up. "There's no need. We'll leave."

After I sign for Dakota and my food, the four of us head for the exit. Just before we reach the door, George yells back at the two old men, "Are you forgetting that it was Indians who the military used in World War II as code talkers? You two were probably there, and us red skins could've saved your asses."

Adraian grabs his arm and turns him to walk out of the building. Once outside, Adrian lights a smoke and glares at George. "You know what, man? Causing shit was exactly the reason we got rid of Butch. Because of him, we'll probably never be able to go back and play at a lot of gigs. I'm the one that got you into this band, and I'm not going to let you fuck everything up."

George looks down at the ground. "I'm sorry, man. It's just that I get sick and tired of always being looked at or judged. None of us did anything to those two assholes, yet still they stared and watched our every move. I'm so sick of that."

All of us can relate to what he's saying, but the way he dealt with it isn't going to change people's minds. In fact, it would probably just make it worse.

I decide to try and make him see reason. "George, don't you think that we felt uncomfortable about being leered at too? Of course we did. None of us said anything because we need this gig. There's not much work out there for us right now. We can't fuck up the gigs that we do get."

"Plus, the best way to combat ignorant behaviours is to do nothing," Dakota says. "Don't let people's ignorance affect you. Let it go. They're not worth it."

"I know, you guys are right, and I'm sorry if I jeopardized us playing at the bar. Next time we get confronted or bothered by people, I won't acknowledge them. I'll just turn and walk away."

Adrian puts his hand on George's shoulder. "There are some times that you have to defend yourself, but always try to either resolve altercations or walk away."

"I know, man. It won't happen again."

Dakota and I say goodbye to Adrian and George and head back upstairs to the room. Once we're sitting comfortably on the bed, Dakota looks at me with curiosity. "Was that true what George said about Indians and World War II?"

"Are you talking about the Code Talkers?"

She nods.

"Yes. It was the Navajo. I think there were initially twenty-nine men who were chosen to use their native language as code so the enemy couldn't crack it. A lot of men's lives were saved because of this tactic."

"That's incredible. Did they get honours for their efforts?"

"I'm sure they did on some degree, but let's not kid ourselves. They were nothing more than Indians, or Red Skins. I don't imagine they received their due respects."

Dakota nods slowly. "But what a cool thing they did."

"True."

"There have been a lot of things that Indigenous peoples have done that we don't get credit for. We came up with chewing gum, oral contraceptives, and medicines long before the white man colonized North America."

Dakota smiles. "You're teasing me."

"I'm not. Look it up. We even created a form of mouthwash."

She laughs. "Seriously?"

"No kidding. It was made from the gold thread tree. And the mouthwash didn't just fix bad breath, but also helped with mouth pain."

"Wild. I don't know if I'm more surprised to learn these things, or that you knew about them."

"My mother is huge on tradition and historical facts regarding indigenous peoples. That's why she's always ragging on me if I miss an event on the rez. She wants me to keep myself rooted in our culture."

Dakota nods. "I think that's good, though. Too many of our people lose connection with our traditions and culture nowadays."

"I know. And I am interested in staying connected. I just don't always have the time to attend every event. I'm working on the band every day. I have very little spare time right now."

"Speaking of your band, do you think there will be any repercussions after George lost it in the café?"

"I don't know. I sure hope not. The whole reason we got rid of Butch was because he was causing problems and getting our asses canned and banned. I really never thought George would act out like that. I thought our problems getting bookings were a thing of the past. I guess not."

Dakota looks concerned. "What can you do about it?"

"Right now, I honestly don't know. In a way, I think that the best thing may be to cut bait and run."

"What do you mean?"

I tell her about how Joe solicited the two of us to the musicians wanted page, and how at first I was opposed. But now, with hitting so much resistance getting a reliable and normal bass player, maybe I should look into branching out, at least to test the waters.

Dakota nods. "You know, that may not be such a bad idea. It sucks that you have to walk away from your band, but if George turns out to be a problem, he will only ruin your reputation further. Then, maybe after playing with another group for a while, you can start a band yourself again. A new one, with a clean slate."

I smile. "I like the way you think."

She moves closer to me, then puts an arm around my shoulder. "And, if you get lonely while on the road playing new gigs, I can always come and visit you."

I lean toward her, and am just about to kiss her plump, moist lips when I'm interrupted by a loud knock. I sigh, walk across the floor and open the door.

"Joe. Dude. You seriously have the worse timing, man."

"It's important that I talk to you. I've just heard about George's outburst in the café. I can't believe he behaved that way."

"Yeah. I know. I was there. Did Adrian tell you?"

He shakes his head. "I went to get breakfast and asked the waitress if anyone else from the band had been in already. That's when she filled me in on what happened. I knocked on both George and Adrian's door, but they weren't around."

"I don't know where they are, but there's no real point of bringing it up with George. I've already addressed it."

Joe looks past me into the room and sees Dakota sitting on my bed. "Oh. Sorry to disturb you, man. I'll just say one more thing, and we can talk more when you're not so busy."

"What's up?"

"While I was having my breakfast, I looked up that musicians site on my phone. You're not going to believe this, but the band that was looking for pro players messaged me and asked if I could send a quick video of you and I playing."

"Two separate videos?"

"Yeah. I guess so."

"How are we going to do that?"

"I already sent the videos we took a while back, while we were rehearsing at home. The Moby Dick bit solo that you played, then the video of me playing that Yngwie solo. I really think those two videos show our talent the best."

I shake my head. "Why didn't you let me choose what to send them? I think there are way better videos that showcase my talent." I sigh. "But, whatever. I doubt they're going to choose either one of us. I went onto that site and saw how many musicians replied to that post. Why would they choose us?"

Joe scoffs. "Because we're fucking awesome!"

Dakota hears this and laughs. "Yeah. And very confident, too."

* * *

After Joe left, Dakota and me finally got our first kiss, one like none I had experienced before. Her lips are soft and supple.

Chapter 6

Country music surrounds us as we wind our way through the almost-full bar. There's a small one-seater table that's vacant right next to the edge of the stage.

Dakota is wearing tight blue jeans and a form-fitted AC/DC t-shirt. She's wearing just the right amount of make-up that accentuates her natural beauty and doesn't cover it up.

I look at Joe and nod, as I do before every set. However, this time, he looks away. *That's weird. I wonder what's up his ass.*

The first set goes great, with bar patrons singing as we play and clapping and cheering at the end of each song. Adrian and George are totally energized and hopping around the small stage, but not Joe. He seems pissed off and detached.

At the end of the first set, I get up from my kit and am just getting off the stage when I see Joe beeline for the exit. Usually we stick together on our breaks, but for whatever reason, he doesn't want to be around anyone.

I spend the next half-hour sitting close to Dakota. She's smiling and radiant. I notice quite a few of the males in the bar ogling her. I'm sure she's used to it.

The next two sets go over without a hitch. The energy is great in the bar and the band plays very well. When we finish the night, Dakota and I run upstairs, where I get changed, then give her a quick kiss before heading back down to the bar to load up the gear with the guys. The four of us pack gear and wrap cords as fast as we can, then load everything into the van. An hour later, we're ready to leave in the morning.

On the way back up the stairs, I ask Joe what's been eating at him. At first he denies it, but after I persist in knowing what the problem is, he tells me to come into his room for a moment. We say goodnight to Adrian and George, and then go into Joe's room.

Once the door is closed, I cross my arms and look at him. "Okay, man. Spit it out. What's the issue with you?"

Joe won't look directly at me. Instead, he stares at the floor. "It's really nothing. I don't even really care about it."

"Care about what? You're not making any sense."

He takes a deep breath, then slides his phone out of his pocket. After taking a few minutes to look something up, he passes the cell to me. I see a private email addressed to him. "What is it you want me to see, Joe?"

"Just read it."

I look back down at the phone and begin reading. I don't recognize the name of the sender, but instead of asking Joe who the letter is from, I read on.

"Hi, Joe.

Thanks for your reply to our ad. Me and the bass player watched your video, and your friend Ray's, too. We were very impressed by both of your talents, but we've unfortunately decided that Ray, the drummer, is who we are the most interested in at this time. I'm including my cell number and email address if you would kindly pass my info on to him.

Thanks for your submission. Wishing you all the best.

Keep Rockin',

James and Leroy."

As I finish reading, I feel both elated and terrible. I can't believe that they're interested in me after only seeing that crappy vid of me drumming. On the other hand, it was Joe who signed us both up to join the pro band. Now, I have an opportunity and he has nothing.

I hand Joe his phone. "I'm so sorry, man. It would have been so cool if we were both chosen. I've never been in a band without you. A big part of me wants to write and tell them that I won't even try out for the band if they don't let you try out, too."

"Oh, great. That would really help me feel better. No thanks. I want to audition for them because they like my playing, not because my friend has to beg them to let me try out."

"Dude. I'm sorry. They could've easily chosen you over me. Maybe they already had a guitar player in mind."

"Not likely. They still have the ad up."

"Do you want me to tell them that I won't go?"

Joe looks me in the eyes. "That depends. Do you want to try out for them?"

"Well, after the incident with George in the café this morning, I don't think this band is destined for anything great. We don't know any other bass players, and we can't afford to get any more bad press. This band is on its last legs. I think it's time to pack it in."

"Answer the question, Ray."

"Okay. Yes. I do want to try out for that band. I have no idea, after they see me in person and hear me play, if they'll want to hire me, but at least it's a shot."

Joe scoffs. "Yeah, a shot you wouldn't have if it wasn't for me."

"Hey. I never told you to sign me up for anything. You did all of that without my say so, and completely behind my back. When you told me what you did, I was pissed. So don't make it like this whole thing was my idea. If something comes out of any of this, good or bad, it was your doing."

"Yeah, Ray. You're the victim in all of this. Seems to me like you're the only one winning."

"You don't know that yet. I haven't even contacted them. Plus, it completely depends on when and where they want me to meet with them. I'm broke, and if they want me to go to Toronto or Vancouver, I'll never be able to afford it. I'm not counting my chickens before they're hatched."

"All right, well, I think we're done talking about it. I'll send you a screenshot of the email so you can take it from there. I'd like to go to bed now, so, if you don't mind leaving."

I shake my head and walk out of his room. As I walk down the hall, I can't help but feel a bit of excitement. I just wish Joe wasn't so disappointed. That being said, it was his idea, and I have no control over who they like.

When I enter my room, I see Dakota with her hair up, sitting with her back against the headboard and watching TV. She smiles, lighting up the dark room. "I thought you got lost or something. You've been gone for a long time."

I apologize, then sit beside her on the bed. I put my arm around her and fill her in on everything Joe just told me. She kisses my cheek, giggles with excitement, and tells me how wonderful this opportunity could be. I nod, then explain why Joe was such a stick-in-the-mud all night.

"He didn't get chosen to audition?"

I shake my head.

"And how would you have felt if he had been chosen and not you?"

"I would've been happy for him. Maybe a tiny bit jealous, but mostly happy."

"That would be a normal reaction for anyone if they heard about something good happening to someone they know. So, his bad reaction kind of reflects on his character, don't you think?"

"I don't know about that. Joe and I go back a long time. As far as I know, he has a good character. Still, even though he blabs a lot, he never really mentions how he feels about things."

"Until now."

"Yeah. Until now."

Dakota and I spend the first part of the night kissing and snuggling, which leads to heavy petting and inevitably full-on sex. I try and make it last so I can please her, but I'm too turned on; her body is like a statue, perfect in every way. Before I know it, the game is over, not long after it had begun.

Thankfully, she's kind about my lack of staying power, and says that it's "no big deal." I laugh and tell her that the last thing a guy wants to hear about his tally-wacker is that "it's no big deal."

* * *

With the five of us crammed into the van and on the highway, Adrian and George decide to get into a battle over the stereo.

George wants to listen to Redbone, whereas Adrian is hellbent to put on a Creedence album. After an hour of listening to them squabble like teens, I finally tell them both that the stereo will remain off for the remainder of our trip. Dakota laughs and rolls her eyes.

We stop for a bite to eat when we pull into Yorkton. Joe points out a small restaurant with a paint-chipped sign that promises all meals under $10.

At the table, Dakota brings up the powwow and asks if we're all going. Everyone but Joe has plans to attend. When Dakota asks Joe why he doesn't want to go, he tells her that he expects Butch to show up at the event, and he hates his guts.

"Who doesn't?" Dakota asks. "That's hardly a reason to miss the powwow."

Joe shrugs off her comment and continues eating his hamburger.

Back in the van, George and Adrian start on each other about music again, and after a while, Joe snaps, "You two are behaving like idiots. It's no wonder Ray is quitting the band."

I'm so stunned, I almost swerve off the road.

Both George and Adrian stop arguing and turn their sights on me. "What the hell is he talking about, Ray?" says Adrian.

"Well, I...I might have a position as a drummer in another band. I don't know yet.

As of now, they have only expressed interest in me, that's all."

I look in the rearview mirror and see Joe grinning, like he's proud of the shit he just caused.

What a shit heel he is for saying what he did. His jealousy must be really consuming him to do such an ignorant thing. I'm amazed—I've never seen this side of him before, and I don't like it.

I wish like hell we weren't all living together right now. They're all showing a new side to themselves I never knew existed.

I feel sorry for Dakota. She thought she was coming to witness a cool band and to get a taste of what life is like on the road. I just hope she still wants to talk to me after all this bullshit.

Maybe when we stop for gas next, I'll call my mother and see if I can crash at her house for a few days. There, I'll contact the new rock band guys and see what they need me to do for the audition.

* * *

We're all bagged out and road worn by the time we reach the house. Everyone piles out of the van and slowly unloads the gear and instruments. Dakota helps me with my lighter drum cases and we load them into my room. Normally after a gig I would put everything back into the rehearsal room, but considering the dynamics of the band, I can't even see myself wanting to jam with these guys again.

I quickly grab some fresh clothes, and Dakota and I head to the rez. I called my mom from Saskatoon, and she was all to happy to have me stay with her.

I reach over and put my hand on Dakota's lap. "Sorry about the hell-ride. Don't ask me what's gotten into those guys. They behaved like little children. It was so embarrassing."

She smiles. "Nah. Don't be embarrassed. It wasn't you that was acting like a jerk."

"I'll drop you off at your aunt's and then head to my mom's. You can call there anytime you want to. She sleeps like a rock, so the phone won't wake her."

"How long are you going to be there for?"

I shrug. "I don't know. She'll probably want me to go to the powwow with her in a few days, so maybe I'll stay on the rez until that's over."

"Do you think she'd be okay if I came over and visited tomorrow?"

"Of course. She's very open to having company. I'm sure she'd love to get to know you."

I pull up in front of Dakota's and after sharing a long, steamy kiss, we say good night. I watch as she walks to the front door, then looks back and shoots me that beautiful smile before disappearing inside.

* * *

A warmer morning wind creeps into the small gap in my window and fills the room with fresh, crisp air. I can tell by the scent of the trees and the freshly uncovered ground that winter is coming to an end. Melted snow forms puddles on the narrow dirt roads, transforming the terrain into one big obstacle course—the first melt of the year.

I take my coffee onto the front step and close my eyes so I can hear what Mother Earth is saying around me. The bird songs are livelier and more purposeful than they have been over the colder months. The wind is calmer now and almost silent as it passes through the spruce trees. Soon spring will be here, and the land will offer a bounty of gifts.

It's why I always preferred spring to any other time of year; it is a time of rebirth and beauty. People on the rez benefit the most, as the flowers and plants are harvested for their invaluable properties in medicine and food. Over the past years, a lot of white people have taken an interest in native remedies and have been buying herbs and other plants from local medicine people. It's funny how our culture was once seen as ridiculous, and now that naturopathic medicines are so popular, our remedies are respected and in-demand.

I hear my mother calling from the kitchen and turn and walk back inside.

She looks up at me. "I see the snow is all melting. I hope you brought your rubber boots and not just your runners."

I smile and shake my head. Same old Mom.

I join her at the table, where we sit and chat about everything that has been going on. After she learns about my opportunity to audition for a new band, her eyes light up. "This is it. I can feel it. Great things are going to happen for you, son. But don't let any more time pass before you contact them. What if they decide on someone else in the meantime?"

"First of all, Mom, don't put the cart before the horse. We don't even know yet what's going on. What if they want me to fly somewhere for the audition? I don't have money for a flight, especially on short notice. Plus, I'm sure that there are tons of great drummers they're trying out. What makes you think they'll choose me? I'm a nobody. I've never even played an A-room before."

"I can't believe you're talking like this. You're a great drummer. You've always had natural talent. The only thing that stands between you and a great career is exposure. You just need the right people to see you, is all."

I smile. "Always the optimist, Mom."

"Never mind that. I want you to call or email them right now."

I slide my phone out of my sweatpants pocket and look up the text from Joe.

Underneath the contact email, I see a cell number. I take a deep breath, then walk into my mother's room—the quietest room in the house—and sit on the bed.

Anxiety rises up in me when a guy answers.

I clear my throat. "Hello. My name is Ray. I'm the drummer from Manitoba who you wanted to speak to."

"Oh. Hey, man. I'm James, the founder and the singer for Red Sun. Leroy, the bassist, and I liked your short vid. You've definitely got chops."

"Thanks so much. I've definitely heard of your band. You guys have a huge following on social media."

"Yeah, we've been around for a long time."

He goes on to tell me that they'll be doing an album in a few months and they have been desperately searching for a guitar player and drummer. He mentions that they've already tried out a number of musicians, but none have fit the band.

I ask him where the band is based out of. He tells me that they're in Toronto.

I swallow. "So, you would want me to come there and audition?"

"Yeah, man. We have a couple other drummers that are flying in from Vancouver and Calgary as well. We need to see the three of you and make our choice so that we can start rehearsals before we go into the studio."

My head is spinning. James is in a much higher realm of professionalism than I've ever known. I'm feeling intimidated and way out of my league. There's no way he would ever pick me over city players from Calgary or Vancouver. I'm sure those drummers could outplay me in their sleep.

"James," I say. "I've got to tell ya, man, I just don't have the funds to fly to Ontario for an audition, then home again if it doesn't work out. Gigs have been pretty sparce up here, and with the cost of living and everything—"

"Don't worry about it," my mother whispers loudly, suddenly in the doorway. "I'll get the money. Tell them you'll be there."

I shake my head and wave her away.

"Okay," James says. "I'll tell you what. See what you can do today and give me a call around dinner time. If you can't make it, I guess it wasn't meant to be. That being said, Leroy and I would love to have you try out for the band."

After I hang up, I sit for a moment to try and centre myself. James sounds like a cool guy, very down-to-earth. I'd love it if it were possible to meet him in person, even if I didn't make the band, which I'm sure I wouldn't. It would still be great to talk with him face to face, maybe get some advice about touring and who to contact for bigger bookings.

My mother is still in the doorway, hands on her hips and looking stern. "What the hell are you doing? Are you purposely trying to sabotage yourself? Call him back right now and tell him that you've found the money to go."

"Mom. I don't have the money, and neither do you. It will be expensive to fly, and then there's the hotel—"

"No, I don't have the money, but come hell or high water, I'll find it."

"I don't want you to borrow money for me, Mom. That's out of the question."

"I didn't ask for your permission." She disappears from the doorway.

A few seconds later, I hear her talking in Cree to someone on the phone. I can understand the odd word—*hello, goodbye*, and a few other commonly used words—but other than that, I'm lost with the language. Unfortunately, many people my age don't understand it. Even with my limited knowledge, I can still pick up on what Mom is talking about on the phone. I hear the word *soniyaw*, which, if my memory serves me right, means money, or something to do with it.

How embarrassing. Everyone on the rez is linked into each other. If there is gossip worthy news, it spreads like wildfire. Whoever my mom is speaking with will undoubtedly spread the word that my mother is trying to raise money for me, her pathetic broke son. As much as I appreciate her trying to help, I'd rather not go than be a charity case on the rez.

Finally, after making a half dozen calls, she comes back into the room. "Okay. Call that band guy back and tell him you will be there for the audition. I got your money for you."

I stare at her in disbelief until she raises her voice, snapping me out of my daze. "Did you hear me, Ray? Call that guy back before he gives your audition to someone else."

"But he said to call him later, around dinner—"

"Call!" She turns and walks back toward the kitchen.

I take a deep breath, then dial the number. As James's phone rings, I hope that whoever promised to loan my mom money actually follows through. Otherwise, I'm going to look like a complete idiot.

James answers the phone on the second ring. When I tell him that I found a way to come to Toronto and try out for him and his bassist, he sounds really enthused and happy. He tells me to try and book a flight for Tuesday of next week, four days from now. I say I'll be in touch when I know my itinerary.

As soon as I'm off the phone, anxiety sets in. I can't believe I'm actually flying to Toronto to audition for an A-list band. I must be crazy to go that far and spend a lot of borrowed money just to get rejected.

For a split second I think about texting James back and cancelling, until I hear my mother coming up the hall. She's too gung-ho about me going. She'd never let me live it down if I didn't at least try to get the position.

"Well?" she demands. "Did you call him to say that you are going?"

"I did. Unfortunately he already hired another guy, someone who's mother isn't controlling."

"Very funny, Ray. When do you leave?"

"Well, if there's enough cash for a flight on such short notice, he wants me there on Tuesday."

She smiles and rubs her hands together. "This is going to lead to wonderful things for you. I can feel it."

I shake my head and smile. "Like I told you before, Mom. Don't get too excited until we know for sure that I got the job."

She disregards my words and instead mentions how all her friends, including the chief, are going to transfer what they can afford into her account. "That's why you have to try your best, son. So many people are rooting for you."

"Thanks, Mom. I'm sure that will help alleviate the pressure."

She laughs, then waves at me to follow her into the kitchen, no doubt to eat breakfast. I swear she was an Italian mother in her past life. She's always cooking and encouraging people to eat until they burst. When I left home, I was at least twenty pounds overweight. It took me a good six months of walking and watching what I ate to lose the fat gut I had.

Just as I sit down at the table, my cell rings. Considering the last person I spoke to was James, my first thought is that he's calling back to say they've found another drummer, one more qualified. Reluctantly, I slide my phone out of my pocket and look at the screen. I breathe a sigh of relief when I see Dakota's number.

I stand up and tell Mom that I'll be back in a few minutes. The last thing I want is for her to eavesdrop on my conversation.

Once in the bedroom and out of earshot, I sit on the bed and answer the call. "Hey, beautiful. How are you?"

"Hi. I know it's kind of early, but I really wanted to hear your voice."

"I'm glad you called. It's been a pretty exciting morning so far. Talking to you is like the cherry on top."

She giggles sweetly at the compliment, then asks me what's been going on. I tell her about going to Toronto in four days to try out for the band. She sounds thrilled with the news. "Do you think we'll get to spend any time together before you leave?"

I tell her that I'll have to spend some time practicing my drums over the next few days, but other than that, I'll spend as much time as I can with her.

We talk for a few more minutes until I hear my mother yelling for me to come and eat. Dakota and I agree to talk later and I hang up.

Back in the kitchen, my mom asks me who I was talking to. As much as I don't want her to probe into my new relationship with Dakota, there's no point in keeping it secret if I want to invite her over.

I divulge who I was talking to, and my mom smiles as she sets the bowl of porridge in front of me. "Gee. Maybe this will be a double whammy of good fortune. First you'll get hired by a reputable band, and then you will move back home onto the rez to be closer to your girlfriend."

I shake my head. "Mom. I never said that she was my girlfriend, and there's no way I want to move back onto the rez. I told you before, I can't concentrate here. There are too many interruptions."

My mother grins. "Don't forget, Ray. I saw Dakota when she was here with her aunty. She's a very pretty girl. If I were you, I would try to stay as physically close to her as you can, or someone else might snap her up."

* * *

The front door is ajar when I walk up the front steps to the band house. As I walk inside, I see George heading toward me with all of his gear.

"Hey, man. What are you doing?"

He looks at me sheepishly. "I'm moving out. Adrian and Joe and I talked about it last night. If there isn't going to be a band anymore, I've got no choice but to move back home on the rez. Both Joe and Adrian are doing the same thing."

Just then, Joe walks out of his room. "Hey, Ray. How's it going?"

"Fine. But I'm a little surprised at what George just told me. I guess all of you have decided to move out. It would've been nice if I was included in that conversation."

"Sorry, man. Desperate times call for desperate measures."

Adrian pokes his head out of his room. "We're not paying rent at the beginning of the month, either."

"What? Are you kidding me? The landlord was always so great to us. He never bitched or complained about us rehearsing and making noise and he always fixed things that needed fixing. We can't screw him over."

Adrian shrugs. "Fine. Let him keep the damage deposit."

I scoff. "Whatever. You've all obviously made up your minds. I guess I'll call and let him know that we're leaving on short notice."

I walk inside my room and slam the door behind me. I can't believe these guys. The least they could've done is to prepare me. Now, instead of thinking I was coming back here to practice, I've got to start packing up my stuff.

Someone knocks on my door. I know exactly who it is, and I have nothing to say to him right now. It's Joe. I walk over to my stereo, put on a Rush CD, and turn the volume up high. I amble around my room, then collect my old suitcases out of the closet. After banging the dust off them, I open my drawers and fill up each suitcase with clothes.

Thankfully, all my music memorabilia and knick-knacks are back at Mom's place. Other than my drums and equipment, I don't have much stuff to pack.

After about an hour, I sit on the bed, pull out my phone and call Mom. As soon as I tell her what's happened, she breathes a huge sigh of relief. "I'm so glad that you're coming home. Now I'll be able to make sure you're eating right and that your clothes are always clean."

I feel like a complete loser having to move back to my mother's place. I'm old enough now that I should have my shit together and don't have to depend on her. What a low moment.

"And Ray, don't worry about making noise on your drums. I'll talk to the neighbors and let them know you'll be rehearsing for your upcoming audition. I'm sure they'll understand."

She sounds happy, like she's won a battle. I think she's forgetting about some of the arguments we had while I was living at home. That being said, in some ways it will be better for me to live with her again. That way, I'll always know that she's safe.

After I hang up, I walk out to the kitchen to get a drink of water. All of the bedroom doors are open, but there's no one here. I walk into the rehearsal room. Other than my gear, everything is gone.

After I've gotten a glass of water in the kitchen, I head back to my room to finish packing. When my suitcases are stuffed full, I drag them from my room to the front door and am just heading back to my room when there's a rap at the door. I open it to see Dakota standing in front of me, smiling.

"Hey, handsome."

I shake my head. "You have a way of showing up when I least expect it."

"Your mom called my aunt and told her that you were moving back home."

I scoff. "Of course she did."

Dakota laughs. "Yep. They are a bunch of chatty birds for sure. Anyway, I thought maybe you could use some help."

I step toward her, grab onto her waist, and pull her into me. "I have no idea how someone as amazing as you would want anything to do with someone like me, but I'm so grateful." I kiss her long and hard.

She pulls back. "That was a great kiss, Ray. But before we continue, I should mention that my cousin Willy is outside in his pick-up."

"Why is he here? Did he drop you off?"

She nods. "Yeah. But also, your mom said that you won't be needing your bed or dresser anymore and, well..."

"And Willy needs them?"

"Kinda."

"Well, I guess Mom is right. My room at her place is really small. Plus, I do already have a bed and a dresser there. So, why not. Go and tell him he can come in and I'll help him load his truck."

She smiles. "Thanks."

I go back to my room to take the sheets off the bed and to make sure the dresser is completely cleaned out. Willy and Dakota soon walk into the room. Willy says hello and I nod back. Then he tells me how he saw Adrian and his relatives driving past with a truck full of furniture.

"I guess you're the last one left here," Dakota says.

"Yeah. I just hope they come back to help me clean up the place. Even though we won't get our damage deposit back, we have to make sure the place is clean for the landlord. It's the least we can do."

Dakota smiles. "You're so different than the guys I know."

It takes us about twenty minutes to carry the dresser and maneuver my bed out to Willy's truck. Once it's loaded, Dakota tells him that she'll get a ride home later with me.

As soon as we're back in the house and the door is closed, we resume our passionate kiss. I'm tired and bummed out about having to move back to my mother's, but here, in this moment with Dakota, all the negativity I feel is fading away. Rather quickly, things

109

start heating up, and we have to stop ourselves and cool down. There's no time for intimacy right now and, more importantly, no bed.

Later, when we pull up to Dakota's aunt's place, I'm just about to lean over and kiss Dakota when she stops me. "My aunt is peeking out her bedroom window. We'd better not."

I look across the front lawn to the living room windows and see no one. Then, my eyes scan a few rooms over and sure enough, there's her aunt's big nosy head, peering through a curtain. "I'm not glad to be back on the rez, that's for sure."

"Well, it's not all bad. You'll be a lot closer to me."

I smile. "Good point."

Dakota says she'll see me at the powwow tomorrow, then gets out of the truck and flashes me her beautiful smile.

On my drive home to Mom's, all I can think about is Dakota, and how enamored I am with her. I wish I could invite her to Toronto with me on Tuesday. Even though I'll have to concentrate on giving the best performance I can while I'm there, it would be great to share the experience with her.

That being said, I doubt she has the money to pay for a ticket. I know I don't. I'm the resident charity case. Oh well. At least I get to see her tomorrow, and I'll make as much time as I can to spend with her when I'm not practicing.

* * *

The smell of freshly baked Bannock and moose steak wafts down the hallway and into my room. Some things I've definitely missed about living at home.

"Are you finished unpacking yet?" my mother hollers.

That's one thing I haven't missed—being in the middle of something and her hollering for me.

"Did you hear me?"

"Yes. Just give me a few more minutes and I'll—"

"No. Come now, or your dinner will get cold."

I shake my head and laugh. *Yep. I'm definitely home.*

Mom and I sit and chat, mostly about Dakota. I want my mother to get used to the thought of her. That way, it won't be such a surprise when I ask if she can come over a lot between now and Tuesday.

After dinner, I help my mother do the dishes, then spend an hour setting up my drums in the front room. Thankfully, Mom has spoken to the neighbors and everyone is cool about me practicing.

As soon as I start to play, Mom opts to go over to Mabel's to play some cards. Something tells me that she's not as into a card game as she's into saving her hearing.

By the time I play my best solo about fifteen times, I'm sweating and my hands are sore. I head to the shower to wash off the sweat.

Later, as I lie in bed, I try to think about how I can improve the solo I'll be playing in Toronto for James and Leroy, but my thoughts keep turning to Dakota. I wonder what she's doing right now, and if she's lying in bed thinking about me. I want to call her, but it's late, and no doubt her aunt will hear the phone.

I drift off to sleep, thinking about Dakota's long hair and perfect body. What I'd give to be lying next to her again.

Chapter 7

The next morning is clear, with the sun shining bright through the curtains. The leaves on the trees are still, with no sign of a breeze. It's the perfect day for the powwow.

Powwows are by far my favorite event to attend. Every year, the entire village congregates to the arena, our largest building on the rez. Late that afternoon, my mother hangs onto my arm until we reach the door of the arena, but the second the door is open she spots a group of her friends and quickly leaves my side. She's wearing her nicest Indian sweater, handmade by one of the elders when I was just a boy. It looks new because she only wears it on special occasions.

I spot the chief over by one of the food and drink tables and am just making my way over to him when I feel a tug on the back of my jacket. It's Dakota.

She grins at me. "Hey, handsome. Come here often?"

"Hi, beautiful. I was hoping I'd see you."

She's wearing a form-fitted sweater overtop body-hugging leggings with tall mukluks. Even though there's not a hint of skin showing, she looks sexy as hell.

She reaches up and wraps her arms around my neck. I'm just about to hug her back when I see Butch walking though the door.

Our eyes meet, and he stops in his tracks.

His cousin Billy walks up behind him, slaps him on the back, then leads him over to a group of people.

I wish like hell he wasn't here tonight, but I guess I shouldn't be surprised. Butch never misses a get-together. Undoubtedly he's been drinking, and likely raring for a confrontation with someone. I just hope it's not me.

Dakota puts a hand on my arm. "Don't worry, Ray. We'll just keep off his radar and we'll be okay."

I shrug. "I'm not the least bit worried about him," I lie.

I take her by the hand and lead her over to the chief to say hi, putting as much distance as I can between Butch and me.

Harlan, the chief, looks happy as he shakes our hands, and thanks us for coming. He's definitely the best chief we've ever had. His father was chief until I was a teenager, but he made more enemies than friends. He had an arrogant personality and some said a penchant for booze once he was behind closed doors. I knew him to be intolerable of anyone who dared oppose his views or ideas. Thankfully, his son is nothing like him.

"I heard about your upcoming opportunity in Toronto," Harlan says. "You have a lot of people rooting for you."

"Well, I'll do my very best. I'm sure they have access to a lot better talent than me, but what the hell, hey? It's worth the shot."

"Don't think of it that way. When you walk into that studio, you've got to feel like you are their only choice. Think number one and you'll be number one."

Just then, the powwow dancers walk into the arena and all eyes are on them. I've always been so blown away by the incredibly colourful and detailed outfits. The work that goes into the outfits can take upwards of a year to make. The feathers and pelts of every kind of local animal are beaded and sewn to make gauntlets, and other pieces create the most spectacular traditional creations.

The feathered headpieces and fur-lined moccasins are made by Mabel and her art circle. My mother used to sit in with the craft circle and help until she started getting arthritis in her hands. Now, she supports the dancers in a different way—by being the loudest cheer section she can be. It's why I always move a few feet away from her once the festivities start. I don't want to be associated to her once she starts hollering and jumping around. She's so over the top loud that I've actually had people come up to me afterward and ask if she's been drinking.

She never drinks, but once she gets carried away, you'd swear she's loaded.

"Look at the outfits," Dakota says. "Have you ever been a dancer before?"

"Hell no!"

She laughs. "Why not?"

"I keep rhythm on my drums, not with my feet. If I were to dance, I'd get sued for injuring people. Seriously."

"So what you're saying is that there's no slow dancing in our future?"

"As long as you're feeling brave and wearing steel-toed boots, I'll give it a try. Just don't sue me if things go sideways."

She laughs and shakes her head. "I'll even sign a waver if you like."

A hard slap on my shoulder causes me to gasp and hold my breath. I turn to see Joe standing behind me. "How's it going?"

"Fine." I force air into my lungs. For a second I thought it was Butch.

"Where's your costume?" He laughs.

I look up and down at him. "The same place yours is."

"Did you see Butch? That prick pulled into the lot and just about hit a group of people. What an idiot."

"Yeah. I noticed him. I don't think he's going to cause any shit. At least not with me. If he was still pissed at us, he would've already done something."

"Maybe. Maybe not. If I were you, I'd keep my eyes on him. The guy is a loose cannon." Joe walks away.

As soon as the drumming and singing starts, the dancers begin. I always wonder how they can remember all the steps and keep up the high energy as they dance in a large circle in the arena. Even though our tribal songs move me, there's no way I would ever have the stamina to dance as hard and as long as they do.

When the first song ends, the everyone claps except for my mother, who is hollering and cheering from the other side of the massive room. Dakota points to my mother, then looks at me. "Maybe she should be in a band. She'd make one hell of a lead singer."

"Everyone around her would go deaf."

As the next song starts, I scan the room for Butch. Joe was right. It's a smart idea to keep eyes on him. That way he can't sneak up on you.

Dakota tells me that she's dying for a drink, so I grab onto her hand and maneuver us to the back of the arena, where there are coolers of drinks. I grab us a couple cans of pop, and then motion to the exit door. "Should we go outside and get some air?"

She nods and smiles.

Once we're outdoors with the arena door closed, there are only muffled sounds coming from inside, and we're able to hear each other. Dakota puts her drink down on a log beside the door, then wraps her arms around my waist. "I'm so happy that you're going to audition in Toronto. I only hope that once you're big and famous, you don't forget about me." She laughs.

I snicker. "Yeah, right. First of all, I could never forget about you. And secondly, I highly doubt I'll get the job."

"Are you kidding? Of course you'll get the job. You can't think like that. Remember what the chief said. You have to walk into that studio like you own the place. There's no room for self doubt."

"I know. I know. I just hope they're okay with Indians. If either of them has bought into the bullshit stigma about our people and how worthless society has made us out to be, I'll be defeated before I start to play."

"Didn't you tell me that they saw a video of you playing?"

I nod.

"Well. Then they already know you're Indigenous. I think it's your talent that they're interested in, not your skin colour. Besides, have you seen what they look like yet?"

I shake my head. "Nope. But I doubt they're Indian."

"Why is that?"

"Because they've been a successful band. How many A-room Indigenous bands do you know of that play all across Canada? Even if Indian bands are super talented, most don't get taken seriously due to type-casting."

She shrugs. "I guess you're right. That is so unfair."

"True. But that's the way it is. And, until something changes, it's the way it will stay."

Dakota sighs, then shrugs off the heaviness of our conversation. "Let's not focus on all that now. I want to have a fun night with you and create lots of gossip on the rez."

I laugh. "I'm in!"

She smiles sweetly, then presses her lips against mine. As soon as her warm breath touches my face, everything around me disappears. We kiss, long and passionately, as the once icy wind twists around us, creating a private shield.

Our passion is quickly interrupted when the arena door flies open and a group of five walk out. The three men and two women walk to the corner of the building and light up a joint. Dakota giggles and looks at me. "I don't think we need an audience."

I ask if she wants to go back inside, and she nods. The wind is starting to feel cold again.

I grab the door handle and just as I'm pulling it open, Butch walks out. Billy and a few other known shit-disturbers trail behind him.

"Well. Look who we have here." Butch breathes the stench of booze all over us. "A snake and a weasel."

I try to maneuver around him, but he moves in our way, holding the door closed. "Where ya going so fast?"

"Come on, Butch. Leave us be. We just want to go back inside. Okay?"

He laughs. "Why? Is your bitch getting cold?"

I shake my head slowly. "You don't have to be like this. Just let us through. We aren't looking for trouble."

"Well, looking for it or not, you found it, Ray. Don't you hate it when Karma walks through a door when you least expect it?"

"Is that right, Butch? You're my Karma?" I scoff. "Fine. You're my Karma. Whatever. Just move out of the way."

Butch pushes his shoulders back, then rams me with his chest. "No way, man. It's time you paid for what you took from me."

I push against him. "What did I take from you?"

"Well, my career for one, and my bitch for another."

"Excuse me?" Dakota shrieks. "I have never been your bitch. You stalked me. I have always thought you were a creep, and you're proving that right now."

Suddenly, Butch shoots his hand out and wraps it around Dakota's throat. "You wanted me, that's why you were playing hard to get. You loved the thrill of the chase."

I grab his arm and try to loosen his grasp on Dakota.

Billy walks up to us. "Come on, Butch. Let her go."

Butch turns and looks at his cousin. "Back the fuck up, or you'll be next."

Dakota is grunting as she tries to pry his hands off her throat. I'm trying to help her by reefing on his arm, but he's too strong, and nothing I'm doing is working.

People inside the arena, waiting to get out, are starting to push against the door. It's the only thing beginning to weaken Butch. Slowly the door gap gets bigger, and I see Joe pushing to get outside.

I yell to him that Butch is bracing the door, and to push harder. Joe sees the panic in my eyes and hollers to the people around him to push harder. Moments later, Butch's feet start to skid, causing him to lose his grip on Dakota. I yank her away just as a half dozen people file through the door to the outside.

Dakota bends over, grasping her throat. I hold onto her as she coughs and strains to take a deep breath.

"What the hell is going on out here?" Joe exclaims.

I point to Butch, who is smiling devilishly. "That asshole choked her."

Joe glares at Butch. "What the hell is the matter with you?"

Butch laughs. "I was just joking around. She's faking being hurt. Besides, what business is it of yours?"

"They are my friends. You have no right to put your hands on her, or anyone for that matter. You're an animal."

Butch laughs again. "Oh yeah? Maybe I'm a bear, and if you don't shut your mouth, I'll rip you apart."

A young woman walks through the door and sees Dakota. I ask the woman to take Dakota inside, and to tell the chief to come out here. The woman obliges, leading Dakota into the arena.

As soon as the door closes, Butch grabs the front of Joe's jacket and slams him against the wall. "You wanna start something with me?" Butch says through gritted teeth.

Joe stares up at him, the bravery he had a few moments ago draining from his face.

Knowing that Joe's actions are what freed Dakota, I feel compelled to return the favour, or at least try. I take in a huge breath, then grab Butch's shoulder. "Let him go, Butch. Your problem is with me, not him."

In a flash, Butch jabs me in the ribs with his elbow, causing me to let go of his shoulder. Then he hauls off and punches Joe square in the face. Joes head falls forward and his body slithers down the wall, landing in a heap in front of me.

I'm just about to lean down to help him up when Butch latches onto my hair and pulls my head back. My eyes quickly catch glimpse of the ten or so people standing at a distance, too afraid to intervene. A second later, I feel the first blow from Butch's iron fist as it makes contact with the bridge of my nose. Immediately a wave of sharp pain rushes through my head, followed by the taste of blood. All I can hear besides the buzzing in my ears is Billy's voice as he tries to reason with Butch.

Slowly, the sound of the crowd becomes clearer. Then, I hear Butch laugh. "Let's see if I can knock him out with one punch, like I did to Joe."

He tugs at my jacket, then pushes me up against the side of the building and raises a fist. "Are you ready to go to sleep, Ray?"

"You're a psycho," I manage to say. "You get off on hurting people. Something is really wrong with your head."

"Maybe you're what's wrong with me. Maybe the next time you go to screw over a friend, you'll remember this day. I told you the day you fired me from the band that I will have my revenge."

"It's no one's fault but your own that you got kicked out. You drank all the time and raised hell at every gig we had. It's on you, Butch, not me."

He laughs maniacally. "I don't give a shit what you say. As long as you're still performing, I'll be somewhere in the shadows, waiting to fuck with you."

"The band is over, Butch. So, your revenge is futile."

"Yeah, I heard that, but I also heard that you're headed to Toronto to try out for a new band. If I were you, I'd hope you don't get the job. If you do, I'll make sure you don't have it for long. And Dakota wanting to be with you and not me? She's going to regret that as well. She's got to learn that if she messes with the bull, she'll get the horns."

My eyes feel tight, like they're starting to swell. I strain to open them as wide as I can, then focus on Butch's crazy eyes. "Mess with me if you want to, but stay the hell away from her, or I swear I'll—"

"You'll what?"

Suddenly, the arena door flings open, and the chief walks out followed by two men. "Let go of him, Butch," he orders.

Slowly, Butch lowers his fist and releases his grip on my jacket.

The chief walks up to him. They are similar in size, both height and girth. I've heard of situations where the chief had to get in between fights before and has never walked away with a scratch. That being said, Butch is piss-drunk and wouldn't feel much if it came to blows.

"What did I tell you," the chief says slowly, "about showing up at events drunk?"

Butch looks around at the crowd and tries to save face by being cocky. "You told me that I should share with you?"

"I'm sick of your bad behaviour, Butch. Until further notice, you're banned from attending any events on the rez."

"You can't do that."

"I just did. And if I hear about you terrorizing anyone anymore, you'll be looking for a new place to live."

Butch shifts his attention to me. His eyes are squinting and look almost red. "You fucked me over again, hey? I'm not gonna forget this."

Butch turns and slowly walks away. A few people from the crowd follow him up the road as I bend down to help Joe, who is now half-awake.

The chief asks me if Joe and I are all right, then turns to the remaining onlookers. "Did anyone here see what happened?"

Everyone looks at their feet, or at each other.

"None of you saw anything, hey? That's what I thought." The chief shakes his head. "You boys go inside and get cleaned up. I'll talk with you both tomorrow."

"Thanks, Chief," I say, helping Joe to balance as we maneuver our way through the door.

As soon as we're inside the lit room, my eyes scan the crowd for Dakota. I spot a side table and am just moving Joe toward it so I can sit him down when my mother appears in my peripheral vision. I just get Joe seated when she reaches me. "Oh, my God. What in the hell happened to you two?" She's yelling, causing others to turn in horror.

"Mom. It's nothing. Stop yelling. Everyone is looking at us."

"I don't give a damn. Tell me what happened right now."

"Just watch Joe. He's not quite steady yet. I've got to go to the bathroom and clean myself up."

My mother sits next to Joe. "Hurry up, then. When you get back, I want you to tell me exactly what happened."

I can still taste fresh blood, so whatever damage Butch did is probably significant. I just hope to hell that he didn't break my nose. Thankfully Joe isn't bleeding very much, so hopefully he'll be all right.

People look at me with shock as I pass by on my way to the bathroom. Thankfully, the sound of drums ring out, which means the dancers are back on and most eyes will be on them again.

In the bathroom, I take a deep breath to prepare myself before looking in the mirror. It doesn't help. I gasp in horror at the hugely swollen black protrusion on the bridge of my nose. I get closer to the mirror and see that the blackness on my nose is travelling under both of my eyes. That son of a bitch. I look like Frankenstein.

I quickly grab paper towel from the dispenser and wet it in the sink before gently dabbing the blood from my nose and cheeks. When I've done all I can to clean up, which isn't much, I grab more paper towel for Joe, then head back to where he and my mother are sitting.

With my head down, I find my way back to the table. I give my mom the paper towel, then scan the room once more for any sign of Dakota.

"She's not here," my mother yells over the loud drumming.

"What?"

"Dakota. She's not here. Her aunt took her home."

I lean in close. "She's gone? Was she okay?"

"She said she had a sore throat, but she looked okay. Why? Did something happen to her too?"

Just then Joe's brother Slim arrives at our table. He says something in Joe's ear, then walks over beside me and speaks loudly in mine. "I just heard what happened. That bastard is going to pay for what he's done." Slim looks pissed off, but he's built like a teenager. Although he's upset about what happened to his big brother, there's nothing he could ever do about it. Butch is built like a freight train and if he even sneezed in Slim's direction, he'd probably pass out from fear.

Slim gestures to his brother. "Help me get Joe into my car, would you?"

I nod and tell Mom I'll be right back as I grab onto one of Joe's arms. I lead him back outside, and Slim goes to get his car, leaving Joe and me alone.

Joe looks up at my face and smiles. "Please tell me I don't look as bad as you do right now."

I chuckle. "No. I don't think that's possible."

"We can't let Butch get away with this, Ray. Enough is enough. This village has been terrorized by him since he was a teenager. I'm surprised that someone hasn't taken him out yet."

"I don't know, man. I like to hope that one day, he'll get what's coming to him."

"Maybe we should hurry that process along?" There's no joke in his expression. He looks serious.

"You're just angry, and rightfully so. Don't think about revenge. It never works out the way it's planned. One day, he'll pick on his equal, and then he'll learn his lesson."

Joe shakes his head. "And in the meantime, everyone has to walk around in fear of the maniac?"

Slim pulls up, and I walk Joe to the passenger side and open the door. u

Joe clambers gingerly into the car. "The chief said he wants to meet with us tomorrow. I guess I'll see you then."

I bend down and put my hand on his shoulder. "Thanks for what you did to help Dakota, even though you got hurt for doing it."

"I can say the same to you. If you hadn't tried to stop Butch from pummelling me, your face wouldn't look like it does."

"You mean handsome?"

"Yeah. That's it!"

The car pulls away. As I turn to walk back into the arena, my mother comes through the door. "I asked Mabel if she would take us to the hospital in Wakeville, and she said she would. She'll be right out."

"Mom. I am not going to the hospital. No way. I'm fine, it just looks bad."

"Are you a doctor? How do you know that you're okay? You don't look okay."

"We don't need Mabel to drive us all the way to the hospital just to wait five hours to hear that, other than superficial wounds, I'm fine."

"Your nose looks bad, Ray. You need to see if it's broken."

"It's not broken. I can breathe through it fine. Plus, nothing is moving around. Just leave it. If it's still swollen tomorrow, I promise I'll get seen by a doctor."

She sighs. "Fine! But I'm holding you to that."

* * *

The weather pushes against the door, making it hard to close. Mom kicks off her boots and heads to the bathroom. My eyes are watering, partly from walking in the swift wind, but mostly because of the swelling.

I go to my room and slide my phone out of my pocket to call Dakota. Just as I'm about to dial, my mother pokes her head into the room. "I'm making you some tea with

Burdock Root and cedar. It will help the swelling."

"Fine, Mom. I just have to make a quick call. I'll come to the kitchen when I'm done." I hope she gets the hint that I want some privacy.

As soon as my mother disappears down the hall, I shut my bedroom door, sit back down on the bed, and call Dakota.

"Hello." Dakota's voice is almost at a whisper.

"Dakota?"

"Yeah."

"Are you okay?"

"I think Butch bruised the skin on my neck. But other than my throat being a little sore, I'm okay. How about you?"

"That son of a bitch. I'm sorry I couldn't stop him from choking you. I tried with everything I had, but he was hopped up on booze and had a crazy amount of strength."

"Don't be sorry. At least you tried. Besides, it's not me I'm worried about. I heard from a couple of people that you took a bad beating. That your nose is broken and there are bones sticking out of your face."

I laugh, and right away get a searing pain in my face. "What a crock of shit. The rez is full of drama queens and gossipers."

"I figured as much. So the damage to your face isn't bad, then?"

"Well, it's not good. But I'm pretty sure once the swelling goes down, I'll be fine."

"Do you think your mom would mind if I came over and visited?"

"I think she'd be okay with that, but I'd better ask first. She's been flipping out about my face since she saw the damage that Butch did."

"What about Joe? Did he get it as bad as you?"

I tell her how Butch knocked him out cold, and how I tried to stop him. "The last I saw of Joe was after I helped him into his little brother's car. I'll know more about how he's doing when I see him tomorrow. We have to talk to the chief together about what happened."

Just then, my mother yells from the front room that my tea is ready. I tell Dakota that I'll call her later, then head to the kitchen.

My mother pulls out a chair for me. "Sit down."

I sit, and she tells me that the chief called while I was talking on the phone. "He wants you to meet him at the lodge tomorrow at noon. I hope to hell that he's planning on calling the cops after he speaks with you. Butch has a criminal record longer than my body. He needs to be locked up for good before he hurts someone else."

I nod and sip my tea. "What would you say if Dakota was to come over for a while this evening? I can really use the company."

My mother sits down. "You've got me. You don't need anyone else to keep you company. Maybe later we can watch a movie together or something."

"No offence, Mom—I love spending time with you and all—but I'm getting quite close to Dakota, and considering what happened to us tonight, it would be good to see her."

She sighs. "I guess that would be okay. Just don't be doing anything stupid in your room."

"What do you mean?"

She tilts her head sideways. "You know what I mean."

I shake my head. "Honestly. You'll have to enlighten me, Mom."

"Fooling around. Getting naked and having sex. The last thing you need right now is to knock her up and get her pregnant."

My eyes widen. "I can't believe you just said that to me. How embarrassing."

"Well, it's true. If you think that Butch screwed up your band, have a baby. That will completely change the course of your career."

"I beg you to stop talking about this."

She laughs. "Well, it's true."

"So, how about it? Can she come over or what?"

Mom gets up from the table and grabs her cup. "Sure. Just make sure she brings a condom."

"You're not funny, not even a little bit."

After I've drank my tea, I call Dakota and tell her to come over. I leave the part about the condom out.

* * *

She looks stunning, even in a two-piece fleece tracksuit. Her dark hair is pulled back into a tight ponytail, exposing her beautiful features.

I hold open the door. "Come in."

Dakota and I walk into the front room, where my mother is sitting and reading the paper. We say a quick hello, then head to my room. My mother calls after us, "Don't forget what I said."

I shake my head as I usher Dakota into my room, then shut the door.

Dakota gives me a curious look. "What did she mean by that?"

"Nothing. I think she's getting dementia."

Thankfully I have a TV in my room, albeit a small one. If I turn up the volume, Mom won't be able to hear me and Dakota talking. I feel like I'm in junior high again, hiding in my room to get privacy from my mother.

Dakota and I lie down on the bed and I surf through the available channels—nothing is on. Dakota spends fifteen minutes making a big fuss over how bad my face looks. Then, she rants about Butch, and how he's a monster that has to be stopped.

I gently turn her head and look at the thumb-sized bruises on her neck. "Does it hurt?"

"Not so much anymore."

I gently kiss the marks, then her lips. Knowing that we can't do anything risky while my mother is home, we stop ourselves before getting too hot and heavy.

For the next couple of hours, Dakota tells me how she'd love to live off-rez in a small apartment. Something affordable but clean, and far away from the snooping eyes of her aunt. "Do you think you'll move off the rez again soon?

"I hope so. I love my mom, but there's only so much of her meddling I can handle."

"Maybe after you try out for that band in Toronto, you'll have a better idea on what you're doing. It would be great if we were both able to move at the same time. I think you'd make a fun roommate."

Normally if a girl said those words to me, I'd instantly feel as though I'm suffocating. However, because it's Dakota, I'm excited at the thought of sharing a place with her. "Yeah. Unfortunately, I won't really know anything until I get back."

She gently runs her fingers over my swollen face. "Are you worried about showing up in Toronto all bruised up?"

"Yeah. I can only imagine what Leroy and James will think once they lay eyes on me. They'll probably think I'm a shit disturber who likes to get into fights. I can't see them wanting someone like that in their band."

"Try not to think like that. Practice like crazy for the next couple of days and just show up. You have no control over what they decide. That's all you can do. If they don't take you, it's their loss."

I snuggle up to her as we watch old Benny Hill reruns. When it hits midnight, Dakota says she'd better get home or her aunt will call my mother, especially after what happened at the powwow earlier.

I offer to drive her home, but she says she can use the walk, and that she only lives five minutes away. I'm hesitant to let her go into the night alone, despite the short walk, but she insists I rest so my swelling goes down faster. Reluctantly, I abide by her wishes and merely walk her to the front door.

With my mother sitting on the sofa close by, I refrain from kissing Dakota goodbye. Instead, I give her a quick hug and tell her to call me once she gets to her aunt's.

After Dakota leaves, Mom makes me another cup of medicinal tea and we sit together and talk. After about ten minutes, Dakota calls to let me know that she made it home safely. Mom and I finish our drinks and head to bed. It's been a long, painful evening, and I'm exhausted.

Chapter 8

I roll over and look at the time. It's 10AM. I can't believe I slept for that many hours.

I slowly reach up and touch my face, anxious about how swollen my face might have become. Much to my surprise, I can feel the definition in my cheeks and nose. Wow! Mom's herbal concoction really worked. There's definitely something to be said about the effectiveness of Indian medicines.

In the bathroom, I look in the mirror. The swelling has almost disappeared, but I'm still black and blue, especially around the eyes.

* * *

The bright sun casts light on the muddy road. As much as maneuvering through deep potholes of murky water is a nuisance, it beats the hell out of roving on the ice and snow. I pull up to the lodge just in time to see Joe's back as he enters the building. I hope to hell that he doesn't look as beaten up as I do. After I park, I put my sunglasses on, lock up the van, and make my way to the lodge.

Joe is pouring himself a cup of coffee when I walk in. He has a bruise in the middle of his forehead but no swelling and no black eyes. I walk up. "Hey, man. Pour me one, too."

He looks at me, then does a double take. "Why the hell are you wearing your shades indoors?"

Knowing that the chief will probably ask the same thing, I remove my glasses.

"Whoa. Shit, man. Your face looks like it got run over by a tractor."

"Thanks. I was thinking if this whole band thing doesn't work out for me, I can work as an extra in a zombie film."

We laugh just as Chief Harlan walks out of his office and waves us in. We grab our drinks and head in.

Harlan sits behind his big wooden desk. Joe and I sit in two comfy chairs across from him.

He folds his hands on the desk and leans forward, his eyes on me. "You look like you've been hit by a train."

"I kind of feel like I have."

He shakes his head. "First, let me start off this meeting by saying I don't know either one of you to be troublemakers. That being said, this morning I had an eyewitness call and tell me that it was the two of you that started the fight with Butch last night."

Joe scoffs. "Are you kidding me? That asshole attacked me and Ray. And Dakota, too."

"Well. That's not how the witness recalls the incident."

I shake my head. "Chief. You said you know Joe and I have never caused trouble, whereas Butch has been a shit disturber since he could walk. You can't really believe that we attacked him."

Harlan takes a deep breath. "I know. And I'd like nothing better than for Butch to move the hell away. That being said, he does have his defense down pretty tight. The problem is if I call the cops and Butch has his witness sign a sworn statement, you two could get arrested, and Dakota could be in trouble, too."

I stare at him. "What? How could Dakota be in any trouble? He was choking her."

"Yes. But according to his cousin, Dakota slapped Butch and Butch was trying to hold her back in self-defence."

Joe shakes his head in disbelief. "Chief, this is all such a load of bullshit."

"I'm not stupid, Joe. I know it is. But I can't act on what I didn't see, especially when nobody is coming forward to back your story."

I lean back hard in my chair. "That's because everyone who was there is afraid of Butch."

"Yes. That makes sense. But the law isn't going to convict him without evidence. And unfortunately, Butch is claiming self-defence all the way." Harlan shakes his head and sighs. "If I were you, I'd steer clear of him and hope he messes up in some other way, which I'm sure he will. If I see him break one more rule, or if someone actually records him screwing up, I can kick him off the rez. But until that time, my advice is that you two—and Dakota—keep well out of his way."

"It's a small village, Chief. How the hell are we supposed to do that?"

"I know. I know. Just stay close to home. If you attend on-rez events, make sure you stick around family or friends. That way you'll have protection and plenty of witnesses. I'm going to call Dakota and tell her the same thing. As for you, Ray, you'll be leaving for Toronto soon, which will give Butch time to focus his attention elsewhere."

I scoff. "Yeah. Until I get back."

The chief stands and walks around to the front of his desk. Joe and I stand up as well. Harlan puts one of his big hands on each of our shoulders. "If you need to get a hold of me for any reason, at any time of the day or night, just call my cell."

After we leave the office, we rinse our coffee cups, then head outdoors. We don't speak about the meeting; it's obvious we're both disgusted with the outcome.

* * *

When I pull up to the house Mom is standing in the doorway, wearing her apron over her clothes. From the eager look on her face, I can tell she's been chomping at the bit to hear what happened with the chief. I walk into the house and close the door.

Mom follows me into the kitchen and we both sit at the table.

"Well? How did it go? Is the chief going to kick that jerk Butch off the rez? "

I know that once I tell her that nothing is happening to Butch over what he did, she's going to flip her lid, but I have no choice. She's never going to let it be unless I tell her everything.

I take a deep breath, then reiterate everything the chief told me and Joe. As expected, Mom stands up and starts ranting about how unjust we're being treated. "Look at your damn face. How can Harlan think that was done to you in self defense?"

I explain that Butch had his cousin lie for him and will act as a witness. "See? There's nothing we can do about it. Harlan said once Butch messes up again, he'll be off the rez for sure."

It takes a good twenty minutes before she starts to calm down. Finally, she sits back down at the table. "Butch is a menace. A real bully. And I don't know anyone that doesn't think so."

I lean over and kiss her on the cheek, then tell her not to worry. "I'm sure Butch's moment of truth is coming." Then, I get up and go to my room to practice.

Halfway through breaking into the solo that I'll be playing for Leroy and James in Toronto, my cell rings. I look down at the screen and smile. It's Dakota. It's been long enough since we left the chief. I'm sure that he had time to speak with her.

I pick up. "Are you okay?"

"Yeah. I'm just in utter disbelief. I can't believe Butch gets off so easily. I mean, look what he did to the three of us, and he gets to just walk away? There's no justice!"

"I know. But don't worry. Somewhere, some place, things will even out. Luck doesn't last forever and everyone is fed up with his bullshit. He'll meet his match, eventually."

"Yeah, but until then?"

"Just do what the chief says and stay out of his way. And, if you do see him following you again, make sure you call the chief's cell number. Other than that, there's not much you can do. Just make sure you surround yourself with people when you do go out."

Dakota sighs in frustration, then changes the subject. "How are you feeling? Has the swelling in your face gone down at all?"

"Yeah. A lot. The problem is, I look like a raccoon because of the bruising."

We talk for another half-hour, then I tell her that I've got to practice my drum solo. The incident with Butch has already cost me too much time. Now, I've got to get serious.

Chapter 9

Winnipeg airport is a long drive from the rez. Thankfully Mabel's son, Rick, agreed to drive me in my van, then park it at my mom's afterward.

Last night, I was up until 3AM practicing. Dakota came over and had dinner with Mom and me, then the three of us chatted until 11PM. I had to practice hard after, knowing I'd be leaving on the plane in the morning.

Before I left the house, Mom gave me a hug goodbye and an eagle feather for good luck. I stuffed it into my bag and told her I'd keep her informed about how the audition went.

* * *

Just before the plane lands in Toronto, I text James. Then I go into the bathroom and splash cold water on my bruised face.

I have no idea how I'll explain what happened to them. I don't really want to go into the whole story of Butch, a psycho from the rez. They might think all natives are like him, and I don't want to be put into that category. I hate to lie, but to avoid judgment and embarrassment, I think up a few different scenarios about how my face got injured. One possible lie is that I was helping someone build their home and while someone was carrying a two-by-four, I got smacked. Another story could be that I was in a car accident. Both excuses sound a helluva lot better than what really happened.

I wait at the luggage carousel, then grab my bag. James hasn't texted me back, so I decide to walk out of the airport and see if I can spot him in the pick-up zone.

Dozens of cabdrivers line the small lane as people arriving in the city race to secure a ride. I see only a few non-commercial vehicles, parked at the back of the row. Slowly I walk down the cab line, hoping that if James is here somewhere, he'll recognize me from the wayward look on my face.

As I approach the first civilian vehicle, a red Dodge pick-up, I look inside and see an Indigenous driver. That can't be him. I continue to the next vehicle, a compact car with an elderly man driving.

I look around and can't see anyone else who could possibly be James. I turn around and decide to head back to the departure area in case James is there looking for me.

When I pass by the red truck, the guy rolls his window down. "Hey. You looking for a ride, man?" He smiles.

I ignore him. He's probably some weird creeper who tries to pick up guys at the airport. Maybe that's something they do here in Toronto. I keep walking and focus on people coming and going.

"Ray. Is that you?"

I stop, turn around, and stare at the driver in the red truck. "How do you know my name?"

"I just took a wild stab at it. Did I guess right?"

I can tell by the joking look on his face that this guy is James.

"Throw your stuff in the back and hop in."

Once my bags are in the back, I hop into the passenger side and shut the door. "Sorry, man. When you tried to talk to me before, I had no idea."

He laughs. "What did you think? I was trying to pick you up?"

"I had no idea. This is a big city. Maybe that's a thing here."

"Well. Don't worry, Ray. You're not my type...or preferred gender, for that matter."

I say I wasn't expecting him to be Indian. When he asks why not, I don't have an answer. He asks me how the flight was, then immediately says, "Dude. Did you try and get fresh with the stewardess? What the hell happened to your face?"

I snicker. "You won't believe it when I tell you. I was helping a friend with house renos, and he walked in front of me with

145

wooden planks. Spun around and the wood sacked me right in the nose."

James seems to buy it. He nods and tells me something similar happened to him before.

As he weaves in and out of traffic, I glance over for a second, just to make sure I was right about him being Indigenous. Yep. I was right. How the hell did I miss that when he and I were talking on the phone? You'd think I would've picked up on something in the way he talked, but I never did. He sounded as white as any other European.

"We tried out the other drummer yesterday. He flew in from Vancouver, spent a night, then flew home this morning."

"Was he really good?"

"Yeah. I mean, we know a lot of the same people. He plays with a lot of A-list bands out West. But unfortunately, he wasn't a good fit. Too busy of a player—a salad tosser for sure."

A wave of relief rushes over me. With my competition gone, maybe if I play really well, I'll have a chance. At least I don't have to worry about James being prejudiced against me. I'm so relieved that he is Indian, too.

"So, what kind of music do you play?" I ask.

"We're kind of a cross between Redbone and Boston."

"Interesting. I love music from the 70's."

"We do as well. It was just a groove that came easy to us, I guess."

"So, where are you and Leroy from originally?"

"I'm from Quebec and Leroy is from Toronto."

"Is Leroy First Nations?"

"We're both Metis. And you're Cree, right?"

I nod. "How did you know?"

"You said you were coming from Wakeville. The only reserve up there is Cree."

Suddenly, my phone beeps. It's a text message from Dakota, asking if I've landed in Toronto yet. I quickly send her a thumbs up, as I don't want to be rude and text on my phone while James and I are getting to know each other.

For the next forty-five minutes, James tells me about the venues they play at in all the major cities across Canada. Then he tells me how much I'll be making if I fit in the band. It's at least three times more than I made with my own group. Then again, the crappy bars we played on the road couldn't afford to pay much.

Finally, we arrive at a huge warehouse in an industrial area. All the buildings are esthetic and clean and well-lit. When I look out at the grounds, there's not a piece of trash lying anywhere. James parks the truck to the side of the building, then leads me into the warehouse through a small red door.

My jaw almost hits the floor when I look around the spacious room. There are

Marshall amps, a white Pearl drum kit, mic stands, and gear set up at one end of the warehouse. A large dog ambles out of a back room and makes its way up to James.

"Come on, boy." James crouches down. The dog keeps moving forward at the same pace—slow. After much effort by the mutt, he finally arrives. "This here is Killer. He's our guard dog."

"Wow. He doesn't look like much of a killer to me." I laugh. "He looks more like a big old teddy bear."

"Don't let his energy level fool you. He knew it was me coming in. He could hear my truck pull up. Trust me, if it wasn't someone he knew that walked through the door, he'd be going nuts."

"That's great." I'm unable to make the jump between this cumbersome creature in front of us and the fierce warrior that James is describing.

James tells me to take a seat on the long horseshoe-shaped leather couch positioned by the wall. He then walks to the back of the warehouse and disappears into a side room, Killer following slowly behind him.

My eyes scan the decorated walls, jumping from pictures to hanging guitars to memorabilia. There's even a huge glass-covered marquee with promo pictures of their band.

A moment later, James comes back down the hall, another guy behind him and, of course, Killer the Sloth-Dog following slowly behind.

James points to me. "Leroy, meet Ray."

I stand up and shake Leroy's hand. He's a lot thinner than James and has a braided ponytail that goes down to his waist. He's fairer skinned than both James and me but has unmistakable Indigenous facial features. He looks at my black eyes but, unlike James, doesn't comment.

Leroy is soft-spoken and asks how my trip was, then thanks me for coming all this way. "Are you tired?"

I shake my head. "No. I'm too amped up and a little nervous."

James chuckles. "Don't worry, man. You don't have to play tonight if you don't want."

"Actually, I'd rather get it over with now, if that's okay with you guys."

Leroy shrugs. "All right. If you're sure."

James points at the kit. "Go to it."

On the walk to the drum kit, I remind myself of what James said about the other drummer who tried out before me. How he was too busy of a player. I make a mental note not to show off and, instead, show my skills through timing and technique.

With both James and Leroy standing and staring, I sit down on the stool, take a deep breath, then start the solo that I should have rehearsed more.

It takes about three minutes of me playing before James raises his arms for me to stop.

Oh no. Was I that bad? I thought it sounded pretty good, considering I've never played this kit before. "s something wrong?"

Leroy looks at James, and James nods once. "No, man. We don't need to hear any more."

I sigh. "Sorry, guys. I could've played a lot better, but I wasn't familiar with the kit and the stool was too low and—"

"Relax, Ray. You're in."

"Huh?" I'm wondering if I heard him right.

Leroy walks over and pats me on the shoulder. "You got the job."

"Are you serious? Are you sure you don't want me to play anything else?"

James shakes his head. "Nope. This morning we watched the video you sent in again. We were pretty sure that you were our guy, but just needed to hear you play a bit here before we decided 100%."

"Wow. This is really great! I mean...I totally thought it was a long shot, trying out. I'm completely dumbfounded right now." I can't keep the smile off my face.

"I think you'll be a great addition to the band. Just, when we play live, maybe tone down the eye makeup a bit."

I laugh. "Don't worry. I don't plan on getting any more black eyes in the near future."

* * *

The hotel room is middle-of-the-road quality, no bells and whistles, but certainly a class above some of the wrecks I've stayed at while gigging up North.

Leroy and James said they're taking me out to celebrate tonight at a club with a live band. Apparently they also want to check out the guitar player, because he's interested in joining the band. I wanted to check into my room first so I could rest and call home with the good news. I quickly look up take-out food joints, then order a pizza. Afterward, I dial Mom.

As soon as she hears that I got the job, she starts laughing hysterically. "I knew it! What did I tell you? I knew you would do great!" Then she starts asking questions, like when I'll be home, and if I know when my first gig will be.

I remind her that I've only just met Leroy and James. "We haven't had much time to discuss the details yet, but I'll let you know as soon as I do."

When she hangs up, I envision what she is likely doing next: calling everyone she can think of to share the news with.

I then call Dakota. For a moment, I think about teasing her, saying that I didn't get the job, but I can't do it. She's been so supportive and encouraging about me coming to Toronto to try out.

She answers on the first ring. "I was wondering when you were going to call."

"Hey, beautiful."

"Have you had your audition yet?"

"Yep."

"And? What happened?"

"I guess I nailed it, because they want me to be in the band."

"Are you serious? Ray. This is so great congratulations! And just for the record, I knew you'd get the job."

"Yeah, I'm pretty stoked about it. However, there is one thing that is kind of a drawback."

"What?"

"Well, now that I'll be on the road a lot more, I won't be able to come back to the rez and see you as often as I want to."

She giggles. "Why? How much do you want to see me?"

"Hm. Every day?"

We laugh. "Well," she says, "what if I come and see you on the road? Is that allowed?"

"I sure hope so. I'm going out with Leroy and James tonight to celebrate. I'll try and squeeze as many answers out of them as I can."

"Where are they taking you?"

"I'm not sure. James said something about going to watch a band. They're still looking for a guitar player, and apparently there's a musician in the band we're seeing that's interested in the position."

"That so cool. I wish I could go and check out a live band with you. At this point, I think I'd do just about anything to get off the rez."

"Why? What happened? Besides Butch and his bullshit the other night."

Dakota's voice drops and her energy changes. "I honestly don't know if I should tell you. You've just gotten such good news, and I don't want to bum you out."

"Tell me what? Did something else happen since I left?"

"It's really nothing major. Just a bit unsettling, is all."

"Tell me, Dakota!"

I hear her take a deep breath. "Okay. But don't tell your mother that I told you."

"My mother? What do you mean? What does she have to do with your news?"

"Well, it's not really my news, it's hers. Your Mom called my aunt this morning and told her that, after you left for the airport, she opened her front door and found a piece of paper on her front step. Paper with a drawing on it."

Anxiety rushes through me. "What kind of drawing?"

"From what my aunt said, your mom described a stick person with a noose around its neck, and the rope was tied to a tree. She also said there were x's in the place of eyes."

"What in the hell? Why wouldn't she have told me this herself? I was just on the phone with her."

"I guess she didn't want you to freak out enough that you'd come home. She really wants you to do well."

I sigh. "Butch. That piece of shit. He's the only person I can think of that would do something like that. I hope my mother has the wherewithal to take the drawing to the chief. Then again, unless Butch signed it, there's probably not much the chief can do."

"I'm sorry, Ray. I debated saying nothing to you right now. I really did. But I know how much you love your mom and I know that I would want you to tell me if the situation was reversed."

Angry and concerned, I tell her that she did the right thing. "I just don't know what else that monster will do to my mom. A while ago she had a huge rock thrown through her window. Now she gets this stupid drawing. It's crazy. But the worse part is, she's all alone in that house. She's like a sitting duck, just waiting for something else to happen."

"Well, I may be able to help there."

"What do you mean?"

"I was thinking that, if she'd let me, I could move into your room temporarily. That way, if any weird crap does happen, I could be there with her and call for help."

"You'd really do that?"

"Of course I would. Like I said, I know how much she means to you. Besides, if I don't get out of my aunt's house soon, I'm going to lose my mind. I swear, she tries to micromanage everything I do. Not to mention the people always coming and going and visiting non-stop. I can't hear myself think most days."

I tell her that she's not only the most beautiful girl I've ever met, but she also has the biggest heart. I ask if she's contacted my mom about staying there. She says she thinks it best if I'm the one that brings up the idea. I tell Dakota that I'll call her right back, then I hang up and call Mom.

At first Mom is taken aback and denies how the note scared her. Then she slowly opens up. "I just don't understand why this is happening. I can't believe how Butch is getting away with everything he's doing. The chief should do something before he goes too far."

When I suggest that Dakota stay with her, she is immediately against it. It takes me a good hour to convince her that it's for the best and it would make me feel better that she wasn't alone in the house while I'm away.

I have just enough time to call Dakota back before I get a text from Leroy and James, telling me to meet them in the lobby.

* * *

The room is thumping with loud music when we walk into the neon-lit bar. Throngs of partygoers stand in front of the stage and dance as the band plays. Leroy points to a tall table at the side of the room, and maneuver through the crowd. Once we're seated, a barmaid comes over and James orders us three beer.

I look up to the stage at the four musicians, all white except for the guitarist. Leroy leans over to me. "The guitarist is rad. His name is Frank. He's done a lot of studio work for great bands. He told the rest of his bandmates that he doesn't want to be in the band anymore, because all they do is covers. He wants to focus more on originals. We're hoping he'll join our band. He'd bring a great sound to our music."

The band is good. I mean, really good. They're versatile, too. In this set they play everything from AC/DC to The Police, and they do it well.

When the singer announces a quick break, the guitarist, Frank, waves at our table, then takes off his guitar and makes his way over to us.

Frank has short hair and chiselled cheekbones. He looks like a contemporary Indian and is dressed in modern, trendy clothes—a tight, shiny button-up shirt with dark, form-fitting jeans. James introduces us and Frank gives me a firm handshake while making eye contact. A good sign in my books.

While James and Leroy talk with Frank, my mind wanders to my mother, and how discerning it is that she received such a threatening drawing. As much as being accepted into this new band means to me, I feel guilty after learning that I'm here while she's at home in a potentially dangerous situation.

At least Dakota will now be there with her. I think about Butch, and what he could do next, and a hard lump forms in my throat. I hope he stops soon, though deep inside I know he won't. Not unless someone—or something—stops him.

After the break, Frank stands up, shakes my hand again, and goes back on stage. Leroy leans over to me and says that Frank is in, so now the band is complete.

* * *

Outside the club, I watch the moon reflect in the glass of the tall downtown buildings. Even though it's late, after midnight, there are people everywhere clamoring to get into small eateries and walking up and down the well-lit sidewalks.

"I was thinking we would take a week or two off, then all converge back at the warehouse for rehearsals," James says to me.

Leroy nods. "Yeah. Frank said he needed a bit of time before he can get together, anyway. Plus, it would give you time to learn the songs."

"That would be great," I say, "but where would I stay while we're rehearsing later on? I honestly don't have the extra cash to pay for a hotel room for any length of time."

James shrugs. "Stay with us at the studio. There are three small bedrooms in the back. I think Frank has a lady in town that he stays with when he's not on the road, so the three of us will have our own rooms."

Leroy nods. "We're pretty easy to get along with. The only thing we ask is that you clean whatever mess you make. That's about it. And, if you have a lady stay over, she can hang out as long as she likes, as long as she doesn't get in the way of band business."

I smile. "You actually allow girlfriends to stay at the warehouse with the band?"

James snickers. "Yeah. But we rely on our bandmates not to bring any nightmare chicks over."

For the entire drive back to the hotel, I'm smiling inside. I can bring Dakota to stay with me at the warehouse. She's going to love Toronto. I do—at least what I've seen of it so far.

When the guys drop me off, they tell me that they'll send mp3s of the songs I need to learn. Then they ask if I'll need a ride to the airport in the morning. I thank them both and assure them that I can easily get a cab. I shake their hands, then head inside the hotel.

I call my mom's home number as soon as I'm in my room. When the line connects, all I hear is Johnny Cash playing in the background. "Hello?" I say loudly.

I hear Dakota's voice as she yells for me to hang on a moment. The music volume lowers, and a few seconds later, Dakota comes back to the phone. "Hello?"

"What's going on over there? Are you and my mom having a rave?"

She laughs. "No. She wanted me to see how she used to dance when she was my age, so we put some music on."

"Wait. What? My mom was dancing. And no one got wounded?"

"What do you mean? She's a great dancer. I even showed her some new moves."

"Are you serious? I'm blown away right now. The last time I saw my mom dance was at a function at the lodge. She did a weird twirl move and knocked over two tables."

Dakota snickers. "Just wait until you see what your mom can do with her body now."

I cringe. "Please don't ever say that sentence to me again."

Dakota laughs, then asks how my evening went. I tell her all about Frank and how he's agreed to join the band. Dakota sounds genuinely excited. "I'm so glad that everything is working out down there."

"I found something else out tonight, as well. Something really exciting."

"What?"

"Just the fact that you can come and stay with me at the warehouse. I'll have my own room, and as long as you don't get in the way of band business, you're more than welcome."

"When? When can I come?" Her voice is bursting with excitement.

"We're taking a couple weeks off, then meeting back at the warehouse to rehearse before we go on the road."

"So you're coming back home tomorrow?"

"I am. I've got to learn some original songs, anyway."

Dakota relays the news to my mother. Then, she gets back on the phone. "Your mom is happy that you're coming home tomorrow and wants me to tell you to have a safe flight."

Chapter 10

Rick meets me at the Winnipeg Airport. He's happy to get away from the rez to pick me up but drives directly to the nearest gas station and tells me that his truck drove on fumes the last few miles to Winnipeg. I pay for a full tank of gas, and we get back on the highway.

I remember when Rick worked at the lodge. He was pulling in good money back then. I knew that, because he always has new everything—new phone, clothes, and a killer stereo in his truck. Unfortunately, he got mixed up with Butch's gang, and quit his job at the lodge in favour of partying. Soon after, he sold his cool stuff. Now he does errands for his mom, Mabel, and works as a gopher for a construction company in Wakeville every summer. I bet he regrets the hell out of getting mixed up with Butch now.

On the way home, Rick talks about when he was in rehab, and how much being there helped him turn his life around. "I wish more younger people from the rez would commit themselves to rehab, but I guess a big reason why they don't is they'd just return to the rez afterwards, and soon they'd fall right back into the same crowd and same habits."

"Why do you think you were successful staying off the booze?"

He shrugs. "I don't know. I guess I saw where my life was going and it wasn't a good place. Plus, my mother is a real nag." He laughs. "I'm more afraid of disobeying her than I am about falling off the wagon."

"I hear ya, man. My mother is great, but when she has her head set on something, look out. I'd rather go head-to-head with a mountain lion."

* * *

A cold chill runs up my spine as we round the last corner of the main road into the rez. It used to be so beautiful here. It didn't matter what time of the year it was, there was always a mystical energy about this place. But now, with everything that's happened with Butch, all of my fond memories of home have been replaced with a lurking feeling of impending doom.

Once we pull up to Mom's house, I give Rick some money for the ride, then grab my bag out of the back and head to the door.

I barely make it up the front steps when the front door flies open and Mom and Dakota are there.

"It's late, ladies. You didn't have to wait up for me."

Mom says that she wanted to stay up so she could make me something to eat after my long trip. Both of the ladies take a moment to size up the bruises on my face.

"Your face is healing quickly," Dakota says. "That's good."

I'm surprised when Dakota wraps her arms around my neck and kisses me in front of my mother. But Mom doesn't even flinch. She just smiles, then heads into the kitchen.

"Wow. You must've bewitched my mother or something. Usually she's weird about any girl showing me affection in front of her. She's old school."

Dakota smirks. "Nah. Your mom is cool. We've become fast friends since you've been gone."

"I'll say. I've only been gone for a day and a night, and already she seemed to have changed her views."

"Not only that, but she said she doesn't have a problem with me staying in your room with you either."

I laugh. "Now I'm sure you did something to her brain."

I put my suitcase in my room, then go to the kitchen and sit at the table with Mom and Dakota.

As I eat the huge plate of spaghetti in front of me, the ladies ask tons of questions about my trip, what Leroy and James were like, and what kind of music we'll be playing. By the look on their faces, I'm not sure who's more excited about the job, them or me.

163

Mom announces that she called a few of her gal pals to tell them my news, which means that undoubtedly, the entire reservation has heard.

After I'm finished eating, Mom takes my plate away, puts it in the dishwasher, then kisses me on the head before going to her room. Dakota and I follow suit, heading to my room together. It feels a little strange knowing that Dakota will be sleeping with me all night and Mom is okay with it.

While we're lying in bed, Dakota tells me how news of the death drawing is all over the rez. "I've had so many calls from people, asking about the picture. Most of them suggested it was Butch without me saying anything. I think he's really starting to gain a lot of enemies, ever since his violent outburst at the powwow. One of my friends said that Butch is a disease that needs to be eradicated before it has a chance to spread and get worse."

I nod. "Yeah. I think I need to go and speak to the chief tomorrow. Even if he gives me the same answer he gave Mom, I need to keep hounding him until something is done about Butch."

I wasn't planning on having sex tonight, not with my mom's room so close, but I couldn't help it. Dakota looked so sexy in her boxer shorts and one of my t-shirts, I just kind of lost control. At least we were quiet...or I hope we were. And at least I won't have to worry about getting up for breakfast and my mother looking at me weirdly.

After making love, I was completely spent and fell onto my back, half asleep. Dakota snuggled up to me, put her head on my chest, and we drifted off.

* * *

The subtle wind affirms the changing season as the trees and foliage come to life.

After spending the morning going over songs for the new band, I offer to take Mom and Dakota to the ice-cream shop in Wakeville for a cone. Once we're off the rez, we stop at the small gas station five miles up the main road.

Mom and Dakota talk and laugh as I get out to pump the gas. A few seconds later, I see Butch exit the gas station with an armful of snacks.

For the first time since I kicked him out of the band, his presence doesn't frighten me. Instead, I feel enraged over the shit he's pulled. Especially in leaving my mother that drawing.

I watch him as he crosses in front of me, unaware of my presence. Then Mom opens the passenger door and tells me to grab her some gum. This gets Butch's attention. He looks at me and stops walking.

"Get the fuck out of here," I say, surprising myself.

He laughs. "Well, look who's back from their big Toronto band try-out."

"I'm as serious as a heart attack right now, Butch. Take off."

"What's the matter, Ray? Are you still pissed over that spanking I gave you?"

"Don't come any closer, or I'll spray you with gas and throw a match on you."

"Oh, really?" He steps toward me. "Why would you do that? In my mind, our feud is over. I got no more bad feelings toward you."

Just then, Dakota jumps out of the van and stands beside me. "Get the hell away from us. You've done enough damage."

"Well, look who showed up. Are you Ray's bodyguard or what? You'd think you learned your lesson the last time I saw you. You'd better watch your mouth if you know what's good for you."

Butch keeps walking forward. I brace myself and get ready to pull the nozzle out of my tank.

"Hey! Hey!" Dakota yells. "Look who just pulled in. It's the chief."

Butch and I both look over at the approaching white suburban that belongs to Harlan. Butch stops in his tracks. Harlan parks at the next gas pump, then gets out of his vehicle. I watch as he catches a glimpse of me, then Butch.

"What's going on here?" He keeps his gaze on Butch. "Nothing stupid, I hope."

"I was just getting some snacks and he pulled up." Butch motions to me.

"Is that right, Ray?"

I slowly nod my head. "Nothing happened."

"All right. Then I guess you'll be on your way, Butch."

Butch smiles, then turns and walks away.

I finish getting gas, then hang the nozzle up just as Mom gets out of the van and makes her way over to the chief.

"That could've been ugly if Harlan hadn't shown up," Dakota remarks.

"I wasn't worried. Not this time."

"I'm not sure if that's good or bad."

Mom finishes talking to Harlan, and he gives a quick wave at Dakota and me before driving away.

Once we're finished and all back in the van, we pull onto the highway and Mom tells me what the chief and her were talking about. "Harlan is taking steps to ensure that Butch gets shut down."

"What does that mean?"

"Not sure, that's just what he told me. And he also said that some of Butch's friends are avoiding him now. I guess they don't want to be associated with him when he finally crashes and burns."

We reach the ice-cream joint and get our treats, which none of us are really in the mood for after seeing Butch. Still, we do our best to distract ourselves. On the way home, our positive energy is restored as we listen to music and sing along.

Once we're back at the house, Dakota tells me that her cousin is picking her up and taking her back to her aunt's so she can pick up some clothes and things. It's great timing, as I wouldn't mind going through more of the songs that I need to learn.

* * *

It's dinnertime when my arms start getting tired from drumming, so I pack it in for the day.

Mom is in the kitchen, making chicken pies. "What time is Dakota coming back? She said that she likes chicken pies, so I made her some special."

"I'm not sure. She left a long time ago. Maybe her aunt had chores for her to do or something. I'll give her a call."

I text Dakota's cell. After fifteen minutes of hearing nothing back, I call her aunt's house number. I expect to hear Dakota's voice when it picks up, but it's her cousin. I ask to speak to Dakota, but the girl tells me that Dakota left for my house over an hour ago. "She had a backpack full of clothes on her shoulder, and wanted to get some exercise, so she opted to walk."

I hang up the phone, then relay the information to my mother. "It's weird. You'd think that she would've texted or called to let me know when she was leaving her aunt's."

"She knew that you were probably busy practicing. She probably didn't want to disturb you."

"I don't know, Mom. I'm feeling a little worried. Her cousin said that she left over an hour ago and was heading straight here."

"You're just being paranoid. I'm sure there's nothing to worry about. She probably just changed her mind about coming straight here and stopped off at a friend's place or something."

"If that were the case, why won't she answer my texts?"

"I don't know, son. But I'm sure you're just getting yourself riled up over nothing."

"Even still, it's dark out now. I think I'm going to take a drive around and see if I can spot her."

* * *

The warm air from today has been replaced with a snapping change of temperature, reminding me that although the ground is pretty much melted, the remainder of winter is still somewhat present.

I drive to Dakota's aunt's, then make my way down all of the side streets. Dakota is nowhere to be found. I spend the next forty minutes cruising past every house with a light on, just to see if I can spot her in a window. I can't see her anywhere.

When my efforts are exhausted, I drive back to Dakota's aunts and reluctantly knock

169

on the door. Soon, I am face to face with Dakota's cousin and aunt. Both of them say they've been trying to call and text her but haven't gotten a response. Again, I ask Dakota's cousin what time Dakota left their house, and what she said as she was leaving. Her cousin tells me the exact same thing as before. "Dakota left an hour before you called. She had her backpack on, and said she was going straight to your place. That's the last I've heard from her."

Dakota's aunt isn't interrogating me this time, as she has done before. Now, she's quiet and has a worried look on her face. "If that Butch has done anything to my niece, I swear!"

I console her, assuring her that I'm sure Dakota will turn up. Then I tell the cousin to let me know if she hears anything. I leave their house and slowly drive back home, watching very closely every shadow or person on the road.

When I walk through the door, Mom is sitting at the table with her head in a crossword book. "Well? Where was she?"

"I wish I knew."

Mom looks up at me. "What? You still haven't found her?"

This is the first time I've seen a look of worry on her since I started raising concerns. She tells me to have a seat, then gets out her small handwritten phone book and picks up the phone. "If she's on the rez, I'll find her."

Hours blend into each other as each call my mother makes comes back with no results. Dakota is missing, and with every passing moment, my heart gets heavier and my anxiety grows. I knew that my feelings for her were growing very deeply, but now that she's missing, I know that what I feel for her is love.

Chapter 11

It's 1AM and despite our best efforts, Dakota still hasn't been located. On the rez, the chief will organize a search party if all other options of locating the person have been exhausted. And at this point, they have been.

Mom calls Harlan, who has already been notified of Dakota's disappearance by her aunt and cousin. The chief tells us that we can join the search party he's organizing if we want to.

"Of course we will join the search party," my mom says.

Time is of the utmost importance when someone goes missing. Usually, if someone has been kidnapped, hope of finding them alive runs out after the first forty-eight hours. This knowledge weighs heavy on my mind. I pray to God we find her soon.

She's so beautiful and vulnerable. The perfect combo for whomever the predator is that has her.

Mom says what I already know in my gut to be true. "If she's been taken against her will, there's only one person I can think of that would have done it."

As Mom puts her coat and boots on and grabs a flashlight from the cupboard, I can't help but think that instead of everyone walking through damp bushes in the dark, maybe we should be focussing on finding Butch.

My mother ushers me out the door. "Hurry up, Ray. Everyone is gathering at the lodge."

While we drive to the lodge, I say nothing. My mind is too busy thinking about where Butch is at this moment. Something tells me that if we find him, we'll find clues to where Dakota is. Dead or alive.

I pull up in front of the lodge and Mom hops out. She looks at me and asks why I'm not getting out of the van.

"I'll be back in a while. I want to check something out first."

"No, Ray. Come with me now. I know what you're thinking of doing, but it's a bad move. Let the chief handle this. In the meantime, we can join the search party. At least we'll be doing something productive and not sitting at home stewing."

I shake my head. "I'll only drive by Butch's cousins house, okay? I won't get out of the van. I just want to know if he's staying there."

Mom sighs. "Okay. Fine. But will you at least walk me inside before you take off?"

I know what she's doing. She's trying to stop a confrontation between me and Butch, but it won't work. I know he's involved in whatever happened to Dakota, and even if he beats me within an inch of my life, I need to look him in the eyes and ask him what he did to my girl.

Reluctantly, I get out of the van and walk around to where my mom is standing. She grabs my hand and we head to the entrance of the lodge.

There are four or five groups of people talking and smoking outside the main doors. People nod as Mom and I make our way inside.

The chief is standing amongst a small crowd when Mom and I walk up. In his hand is a list of the names of people who are participating. He tells us that each group will cover an area around the reservation. "You can come with me, Ray."

"That's a great idea. But I need to do something first."

He tilts his head suspiciously. "Okay. Fine. I'll go with you."

Shit! I force a smile and agree.

Mom goes off to find the group she'll be searching with. Harlan and I walk outside and get into his truck. He starts the motor. "So, what do you have to do? Where are we going?"

I try to come up with something fast and fail. "Never mind. I can deal with it later."

I can tell by the look on the chief's face that he doesn't believe me, but thankfully, he lets it slide. "You know, there's a place just off the rez, a house where a lot of our young people go to party. Maybe we should take a quick drive past there and see if we can spot Dakota, and if not, maybe someone she knows."

I nod. "As much as I don't think she'd be at a party house, it couldn't hurt to check it out."

As we drive along the dark road and pass through the entrance to the rez, Harlan tells me how proud everyone is that I got the new band job. It's funny, but ever since Dakota disappeared, I haven't thought about going back to Toronto once.

As he steers around each dark turn, my eyes follow the headlights as they shine on the sides of the road. I'm hoping to catch a glimpse of Dakota walking home. But all I see are endless trees and dirt.

* * *

Every town has a seedy side, and Wakeville is no different. Harlan takes a side road and drives around the back of the town. Old apartment buildings and shack-like houses appear on either side of a small lane. Harlan motions toward one of the shacks, a small brown structure with the windows boarded up and the door painted black. From inside comes muffled music. "That's the party place I was thinking about. There are always shady characters and hardcore partiers hanging out in there."

As soon as he pulls his truck over, I grab the door handle and am just about to get out when the chief puts a hand on my shoulder. "Wait. You don't want to be getting out of the truck and going up to that house."

"If there's a chance that Dakota is in there, I'm going." I get out of the truck and walk across the front lawn. There's an old ringer washer on one side and garbage bags on the other.

I hear Harlan quickly get out of the truck behind me. "Shit! You aren't that good at listening, are you?" He follows me up to the door.

The ear-busting bass of the shitty music playing inside makes the single-paned windows shake. I doubt whoever is inside will hear me if I knock. Harlan and I stand on the top step.

"This is a bad idea," Harlan shouts. "Who knows what kind of drugs or booze these guys are on. We should go and maybe come back during the day."

"You go ahead and leave. I'll understand."

The chief shakes his head. "I'm not leaving without you, so let's go." He grabs onto my arm.

Suddenly the door swings open, causing Harlan and me to jump back. A blond guy with a huge build lumbers out onto the porch. "Hey. Who are you guys?" The warm stench of booze permeates the air. "If you guys don't want to get puked on, I'd move."

I try not to breath in his boozy breath. "Is there a girl named Dakota inside?"

The guy shrugs. "I don't know. What does she look like?" Then a huge spray of fresh puke blasts from his mouth.

Harlan looks down at his vomit-splashed boots. "Come on, man. What the hell?"

I keep my eyes on the guy. "She's beautiful, petite, and Indigenous."

The drunk sob cackles. "Oh, she's a squaw?"

I reach out and grab the front of his shirt. "A what?"

Harlan grabs onto my arm. "Let him go. He's not worth it."

The drunk guy staggers backward into the wall. "Relax. Don't get your eagle feathers ruffled. I was just kidding." He puts his hand up. "No. There are a couple of straggler chicks inside, older crackheads. Other than that, there are only dudes."

Harlan turns to me "Satisfied?".

"He's probably lying."

"Why would he? Besides, we can't just go storming into someone's house. Come back to my truck and we'll talk about what our next step should be."

Frustrated, I follow Harlan back to his truck. He gets into the driver's side and pops up the automatic lock on my side. I'm just grabbing the handle when an older white Pontiac pulls up behind us.

The driver, a lanky white guy with stringy hair, gets out of the driver's side. Then the two back doors open and from one side hops out a short, fat girl about forty. From the other I see a tall, broad figure step out and slam the door. I focus on him as he walks into the light from the house, and I can see his face.

It's Butch.

Son of a bitch!

Adrenaline surges through me. It's as if I've been electrocuted. Suddenly, all my inhibitions and fears completely drain from my body.

He's responsible for whatever happened to Dakota. I know he is. He was crazy about her. He stalked her. When he found out that she was with me, he tried to choke her out. No one else has an axe to grind with Dakota, except him.

I let go of the handle and turn toward Butch as he heads in my direction.

It takes until he's directly in front of me before he recognizes me. His face splits into a grin. "Hey, look who's here, the little pissant whose eyes I blackened. What are you doing off the rez? Isn't your mommy going to be worried about you, so far away from home?" Butch and his two cohorts start to laugh.

"You piece of shit. Where's Dakota?"

The smug smile on his face quickly disappears. "What did you say to me?" He steps closer.

I hear Harlan as he gets out of his truck. "Hey, boys. Don't be crazy, now. Let's just all go our separate ways."

"Not until he tells me where Dakota is."

Butch scoffs. "How the hell should I know where your cheap-ass girlfriend is?"

"That's it, you crazy piece of shit. You're going down."

Butch laughs. "Are you gonna teach me a lesson? I've got to see this shit."

Without thinking of what move to make next, my arm pushes out at lightening speed and the palm of my hand rams into Butch's nose. He staggers back, and blood spurts out each nostril, dripping off his chin.

He raises a hand and wipes away some of the blood. "I'm impressed, you little pansy. But that was the one and only time you hit me. It's my turn now." Butch grins, and the blood from his nose travels over his lips and colours his front teeth. If I wasn't so enraged, I might be scared at the gruesome sight.

He reaches out to grab me, but I duck out of his way. Butch is strong, very strong, and if I let him get a hold of me again, I'm done for. I've got to fight with everything I have if I want to keep from getting seriously hurt.

I vaguely hear Harlan yelling as I shift my weight, then—with everything I have—

boot Butch in one of his knees. I watch the psychotic madman as he teeters, then drops to the ground, holding onto his leg and cursing in pain.

I quickly glance over at the chief, who looks just as surprised as me that I've just bested someone as big and powerful as Butch. Then I turn back to Butch "Where is Dakota? You piece of shit. Tell me now, or I'll stomp on your leg."

Butch puts one hand up. "Don't do it. I have no idea where Dakota is. I didn't go near her."

"Bullshit!" I holler, then get ready to boot his injured leg.

"Enough!" the chief yells, then grabs me around the waist and pulls me backward.

Just then, I see red and blue flashing lights coming up the small road toward us. The lanky driver of the Pontiac and the stout women quickly sprint inside the house, whereas Butch remains, moaning in pain as he continues clutching his leg.

The cop car pulls up behind us, then two officers get out. Both have flashlights shining on Butch, me, and the chief.

"What seems to be the issue here?" one cop says.

Harlan lets me go, then introduces himself as the chief on the reservation. One cop scoffs. "I don't give a shit if you're the Prince of Brunei. I asked you what is going on."

"These two have an on-going dispute. It's over now. I was just taking Ray here back to the rez. Everything is fine."

The second cop cradles his flashlight under his arm while he retrieves a pen and a notepad from his jacket pocket. Ignoring Harlan's statements, they proceed to gather all of our information. They write down the sequence of events that led us to this point, including the fact that I hit Butch first. Then they put me in handcuffs.

They seem sympathetic to Butch's injuries until they run his name and find out that he's in breech of his probation by being off the rez and breaking his curfew. For him, they call an ambulance, after they put him in cuffs. For me, they toss me into the back of their swat car. Harlan they let go, as they believe he was trying to resolve the situation before things got physical. I yell at him to call my mom as he gets back into his truck and drives away.

We wait a couple more minutes until the ambulance arrives, then they drive me downtown to the Wakeville police station. All I can think about is Dakota, and how much time I'm going to waste at the copshop instead of looking for her.

It felt good to finally take down Butch. Damn good. But any hope I had of getting answers from him about Dakota diminished the second the cops showed up. I should have listened to the chief. I should have held my temper, which usually isn't hard for me, but now that I'm in love with Dakota and she suddenly went missing, all of my emotions are heightened.

For the first time in my life, I get fingerprinted, booked, and told to sit on one of the long, uncomfortable benches. Once I'm seated, the cop takes the cuffs off my wrists, which are behind my back, and re-cuffs them in front of me. "Behave yourself." He walks to the front of the small room and crosses his arms.

There are five other prisoners in the room with me. Four I'm sure I've seen around town before, and one who looks like he's from someplace else. His clothes are trendy, as is his slick hairdo, and he doesn't seem as if he's been arrested before. His eyes are huge and he keeps staring at the rest of us. He looks paranoid and freaked out.

Another officer walks through the entrance doors and stands at the front of the room with the other cop. "Get comfortable, guys. We're short-staffed tonight, so you are going to be here until you get processed. Then you'll be put in the holding cells until the judge can see you, which might be tomorrow if there's enough time."

What the hell does that mean? I thought, once they brought me here, that I'd just have to make a statement or something, and then I'd get released. I'm not even drunk like the rest of these guys—I can't stay here over night. I need to be out looking for Dakota. And my mom will be losing her mind by now.

I nod my head at one of the cops. Looking as if I just killed his best friend, he scowls as he makes his way over to me. "What do you want?"

"I can't stay here, sir. My girlfriend is missing and I'm a part of a search party. Every minute I'm in here, I could be out searching for her."

He laughs. "Well, that's a new one. You should've thought about your girlfriend before you got into a fight." He turns and walks back to the front of the room.

What a complete dick. He spoke to me as if I'm some kind of scumbag. I guess everyone in here is judged the same. We are all dirt, and the cops are the kings.

* * *

A gruelling five hours pass in this institution, but it feels like days. They've taken a statement from me and have taken down all of my information. Now, I'm just waiting to be taken to a holding cell to wait out the time until I can speak to a judge.

As much as the cop that I spoke to earlier was a dick, the rest of the officers seem pretty cool. It's unreal the amount of shit they have to put up with. Half of the guys in this room have, at one time or another, been yelling out profanities and asking for stupid shit, like smokes or something to eat. The abuse and stress that the officers go through is surprising. Other than what I've seen on cop shows, this is the first time I've witnessed cop/criminal interactions.

When everyone but me has been taken to a cell, the main door opens and a wheelchair with a guy in it, head down, gets wheeled in. It's only when the injured guy lifts his head that I see the person's face. *Sonofabitch.*

I can't believe Butch is here. I thought he was taken to the hospital. Why the hell have they brought him here?

An officer wheels him over beside my bench, then joins the other two at the front of the room. I try not to make eye contact with Butch. I know that if I look into his eyes, even once, I'll freak out at him again, and I'll get into even more shit than I'm already in.

I look up at the clock and catch a glimpse of Butch's leg. He doesn't have a cast on it; instead, his knee is wrapped in a tensor, and he's holding an ice pack on top of his knee. He's not moving his injured leg at all.

Good! I hope it hurts like hell. He deserved that hard kick I gave him, and I don't have even the littlest bit of compassion for him.

For a second, I debate yelling at the cops about Butch's antics. I want to tell them how he stalked my now missing girlfriend, how he choked her, and how he beat the hell out of me and Joe. But then I remember how dismissive the cop was who I tried to talk to earlier, and I know saying anything probably won't do me any good.

When the officers leave the room for a couple of moments, and I'm left alone with Butch, he looks over at me with a serious look on his face. "Hey, Ray. That was a nice job you did on my knee."

"I don't give a shit. You deserved it and more. And if the cops hadn't shown up when they did, I would've done the same to your other leg."

"Oh, you think so, do you? You think you're that tough?"

"Shut up, Butch. You're an asshole, and I've got nothing more to say to you."

"Look, man. I know you don't like me, and after you ruined my life and kicked me out of the band, you haven't been in my good books, either. But I've got to tell you something before the cops come back and I won't be able to say shit."

"I don't want to hear it."

"Yes, you do. It's important."

I turn and look him in the eyes. "Is what you have to say about Dakota?"

"In part, yes."

"Hurry up, then. What is it?"

"I didn't have anything to do with her disappearance. I only heard that she was missing right before I saw you at that house. I've done a lot of things wrong, like when I put my hands around her neck and when I pummelled you and Joe at the powwow, but I was high on coke. Even so, I would never kidnap anyone or do anything like that."

185

I look at him in utter disbelief. "Think about what you just said to me, Butch. You just admitted that you choked Dakota while you were hopped up on coke. If you're capable of that, you're capable of anything."

"Wrong, Ray. There are limits to my temper, I promise you that."

"All I know is that if I find out any harm has come to Dakota, you're the first person I'm looking for. And, just so you know, the chief is aware of that little psycho drawing you left at my mother's house. All the shit you've done is finally starting to stack up against you."

Confusion crosses his face. "What psycho drawing, Ray? I don't know what the hell you're talking about."

I snort. "What about the rock you threw in my mom's front window? Are you going to deny that as well?"

"Yes! Of course I'm going to deny it. I never did it. This's crazy. You know my shortcomings—you know the extent I've gone to when I'm under the influence. When have you known me to do trivial things like draw weird pictures or throw rocks through windows?"

"I'm not going to talk about this anymore with you. You're a worthless piece of shit, Butch. You proved that for years when you messed up the band's reputation on the road. You promised you would change, but you never did. You just did what you're doing right now—lying. All you ever cared about was doing whatever suited you. Drugs, booze, fighting. You'll never change, and I would have to be an idiot to believe one word you say."

Just then, two of the three cops walk back into the room, and instantly the conversation between Butch and me ends.

Chapter 12

The ride home in the chief's truck is dead silent. All he says is that he tried to get me released last night, but because of the cops being short staffed, I had to wait longer to see a judge.

The sun is just coming up when we reach the rez. Harlan pulls up in front of my mom's house and puts the truck in park. "You know, Ray. You have a lot of people rooting for you, including me. You're not known as a troublemaker. I'd hate to see you take that road now. Regardless of how sure you are that Butch has something to do with Dakota's disappearance, violence is never the answer. After you hurt him, did he tell you anything you wanted to know?"

I shake my head. "No."

"Exactly. You have to fight with your brain, not your body. That's how you will eventually find justice and the answers you're looking for."

"I know. You're right. I'm not a physical guy, but he pushed me to my breaking point. I mean, how much more am I supposed to take? And more importantly, if he has Dakota trapped somewhere, God forbid if she's injured, she needs to be found now. I guess that's why I lost it on him. I panicked."

"I know you're sure that Butch has something to do with her disappearance, but you have no evidence. It's not like I don't believe you about what happened at the powwow. But as I said before, there's nothing I can do to him without witnesses. And, if you think that he's responsible for Dakota being gone—"

"I don't think he has something to do with her being missing. I know he does."

Harlan puts a hand on my shoulder and tells me that I should probably go inside. "Your mother has been worried sick all night."

I thank the chief for picking me up and apologize for taking up so much of his time. Then I get out of the truck and tell him that I'll talk to him later.

My mother is sitting at the table when I walk into the house. Her hair is scraggly and loosely tied at the back of her head. There are dark circles under her eyes and her face is drawn and stressed. As soon as she sees me, she gets up, races over, and gives me a strong hug. "I've been worried sick."

"I know, Mom. I'm sorry."

We both sit down and I go through the whole chain of events that got me thrown into jail. When I describe how I took down Butch with one kick, she looks almost proud.

Then, her expression returns to stress. She gives me a long lecture, similar to the short one that Harlan just gave me in the truck. I apologize to her, then head to my room to change the clothes that now smell like a piss-ridden jail cell.

Once I'm in clean clothes and have splashed cold water on my face, I drink a fast cup of coffee and tell Mom that she should get some rest after being up all night. I head for the door.

"Where are you going?"

"I'm heading to the lodge to join the search for Dakota."

At first she asks me to stay at home, but I say that I can't sit here doing nothing while Dakota is out there somewhere and head out the door.

* * *

There's an early morning crowd gathered at the front of the lodge. It's nice to see this many people who are willing to look for Dakota. I stand beside Mabel, who has a clipboard and is calling out names and grouping people together for the search. She turns and sees me, then gives me a compassionate look before turning her attention back to her list.

A few more cars show up, and after they park, the occupants walk over and join us. Joe is amongst them. He walks up to me and puts his hand on my shoulder. "Don't worry, man. We'll find her."

Mabel looks at Joe, then me. "You two can search together."

Once everyone knows where they're headed, I turn to Joe. "Are we taking your vehicle or mine?"

"Mine—or should I say, my brother's—was stolen two nights ago. Now that it's gone, I've got to do what I've always done, and bum rides off everybody else."

"That sucks, man. Where was it stolen from?"

"I was at the pub in Wakeville with some friends. When we walked out into the parking lot, the car was gone. Granted, it was piece of crap, but it was the only set of wheels I had access to."

"Any idea who would've done it?"

He nods. "Definitely. It was right after Butch knocked me out cold at the powwow. Since I've never really had any trouble with anyone else on the rez until then, it's only logical that it was him."

I frown. "Wouldn't be surprised."

We drive out of the parking lot and head up the old logging road that runs parallel to the rez. Joe glances at me. "Do you really think we're going to find her up here? I mean, she could be anywhere. Even in the river." Joe suddenly realizes what he's said. "Sorry, man. I wasn't trying to be insensitive. I'm sure she'll turn up happy and healthy sooner or later."

"She has to. I don't think I could live with any other outcome."

Joe tries to change the subject and get my mind off things. "So, tell me about Toronto. Where did you audition?"

I sigh, not really wanting to think about anything but finding Dakota. "It was cool. A warehouse not far from downtown. They definitely have backing. The place was stocked full of awesome instruments and gear."

"Yeah? And to think, I could've gone with you if they picked me. Now, it's just you, and I'm left here in this shithole."

"Come on, Joe. Don't look at things like that. You can easily put your name out on the internet again. I bet you'd find a new band in no time at all."

"Pfft. Yeah, right. It's not like there's tons of opportunities for Indians on the main circuit. You were lucky. You won the lottery. I can't see that happening for me."

There's a bitter tone mixed in with his words. I thought he was past being jealous about me landing the gig and him not.

He sighs. "I mean, not that I begrudge you getting in. I just find it a bit ironic how I'm the one who signed you up, and then I get rejected and my life gets ruined. Meanwhile, you've been instantly turned into a star on rez because of what I did for you. As for me? I'm still the same piece of shit nothing I've always been."

"You know what, Joe? I had nothing to do with you posting my name on that web page. And I definitely had nothing to do with Leroy and James not choosing you. If you remember, I was pissed about you putting my name in the hat to begin with. So, I don't think it's fair that you have resentments toward me."

"Resentments? Are you kidding? I'm just as happy about you getting hired on with an A-band as the rest of the people on-rez are. I don't begrudge you at all."

"Let's just talk about something else."

"Okay. That's cool. No problem." He looks ahead at the gravel road. "Where the hell are we supposed to be looking out here, anyway?"

"Don't ask me. I guess we just keep our eyes open for anything suspicious."

"Well, this road ends soon, just past the landfill, about a quarter mile up the road. I come up here quite a bit on my brother's quad. It's peaceful on this road, just far enough from the rez not to hear any noise."

We travel a few more minutes on the road, then I see a huge tarp over what looks like a large car. "Look at that, Joe. I wonder if we should stop and check it out?" I slow the van down.

He shakes his head. "Don't bother. That's the chief's nephew's car. It's a rust bucket. It's been up here a while now, like a couple of months. The stupid kid who owns it blew the tranny. I guess it was his first car, so he came up here and covered it with a tarp until he can afford to get it towed to the rez. The kid does odd jobs at the lodge. If his drinking habit wasn't his top priority, he might have saved the money already. But the car is still sitting here, unfixed."

"You think we should have a look anyway?"

"Naw. I did already, the other day. I wanted to see if there were any wild animals living in it." He laughs.

I resume my speed as we head toward the landfill area.

"Hey, Ray." Joe looks at me.

"What's up?"

"I'm sorry for my stupid outburst. I really am excited for you. And don't worry about me. I'm going to take your advice and try posting my name on the rock site again."

"You should."

The nasty smell of the dump seeps into the van. Straight away, I tell Joe to do up his window. There's a small clearing where vehicles pull into to unload their garbage. I pull the van in, only feet away from the mountain of trash.

"Should we get out and look around?" Joe asks.

"As much as I want to say no right now, it's a good idea. I don't think Dakota is here, but at least we can tell the others that we've covered this area."

I reach into the back seat and find a roll of paper towel, then rip off two large pieces for Joe and me to cover our noses and mouths. Outside, I do my best to breathe through my mouth so the stench of the place doesn't make me gag.

Joe goes in one direction and I go in the other. My eyes scan the huge piles of trash as I maneuver my way around the circumference. As I walk along, I catch the odd sight of rodents as they startle from the sound of my footsteps and scurry under pieces of garbage. Joe meets me at the halfway mark around the putrid mountain, and we both walk back to the van together.

Once we're back in the van, Joe tells me that he saw remnants of a bear cub, probably attacked by a mountain lion or something.

I grimace. "Or an asshole that thought the cub made an easy target."

"True. There are too many guys I know on rez that treat animals like shit. We're supposed to be all about the land and honouring animals, but things are different now. The younger guys don't give a shit about our culture. They bitch and moan about everything bad that the white man has done to our people, but the truth is, those little punks have no idea what it really means to be Cree."

"I don't think it's just punks from the rez that do stupid shit. I think it has nothing to do with race and culture, and everything to do with some individuals being disconnected with everything. Their families, authority figures, their culture, and, more importantly, themselves."

Joe looks at me and laughs. "That's probably the deepest shit I've ever heard you say, Ray."

When we get back to the lodge, Mom is in the meeting area, talking to the chief. Joe and I walk up and join them just as a reservation police officer enters the building. I know most of the cops that patrol the rez, but not this one. This guy is young, younger than most, and has a serious demeanor about him. Before Joe and I can even say hello to Mom and the chief, the officer asks where he can find Dakota's family. The chief points to a group of people, amongst whom is Dakota's aunt. The young cop heads over to speak with her, the chief excuses himself and follows the officer.

"That's interesting," says Mom. "I wonder if there's been any news about Dakota."

Instead of engaging in conversation, I stare at the cop and the chief, trying to read their faces. I want to walk over and join the conversation, but I can't. It's not my place.

Joe puts his hand on my shoulder. "It'll be okay, buddy. Maybe the cop just wants to ask some questions."

My mother nods. "Yes. It's probably nothing, son. Don't worry."

I watch as the cop reaches into his jacket and pulls out his cell, then swipes a few times. A moment later, he shows Dakota's aunt something on the screen. She immediately covers her mouth and chokes out a sob. The officer says a few more words, then turns and exits the building.

Both Dakota's aunt and Harlan go into the main office and close the door. A sick feeling forms in the pit of my gut and my hands tremble. What in the hell is going on? What did the cop show Dakota's aunt on his phone?

"Did you see that?" asks Joe. "Dakota's aunt just had a meltdown."

My mother looks at Joe sternly. "Be quiet. We all saw. You don't need to state the obvious and upset Ray. Not until we know exactly what's going on."

The dark feeling forming inside me makes my lungs constrict. I have to force myself to take a deep breath as I wait for the chief to reappear from his office with Dakota's aunt.

Mom is right. We shouldn't make assumptions until we know for sure what's going on. That being said, it wasn't good news that the cop delivered. I just pray that nothing too horrible or permanent happened to my girl. I would never find anyone as wonderful as her again.

I can't help but picture her and me in Toronto, at the warehouse, while I rehearse. I imagine us exploring all the cool sights of the city. She kept telling me how excited she was about getting off the rez and coming with me. Without her, I likely won't be able to muster any excitement for my job with the band. What good is success if you can't share it with someone you love?

"Look," Joe says. "Here comes the chief."

Harlan is leaving the office, Dakota's aunt only a few steps behind. Her face is red and her eyes are puffy. She walks back to her group, and the chief heads over to where we're standing.

I speak first. "What's happening? What did the cop say?"

Harlan leans in close, not speaking above a whisper. "The police have some items in their possession and wanted confirmation that they belonged to Dakota."

My mother speaks up. "Items? What items? And whatever they were, did the cop get confirmation from Dakota's aunt that they belonged to her niece?"

The chief sighs and puts his head down. "I'm not supposed to say anything, but since the news will undoubtedly make the rounds quickly, I will tell you. They found a hoodie and a bracelet. Dakota's aunt said they belonged to her niece, no question."

My head is spinning. "That doesn't mean anything happened to her, though. Maybe she was at one of her friend's houses and the items fell out of her backpack, or something like that."

"There was blood on the hoodie. Not a lot, but there was blood."

My heart starts to race. What the hell could've caused blood to be on her clothing?

Please, Dakota. Please let there be a logical explanation for all of this.

Chapter 13

After a long, cumbersome wait for all the search crews to return to the lodge, the chief tells everyone to go home until tomorrow morning, when we will all meet up back here and resume the search.

My mother makes me a bowl of tomato soup, then sits beside me. Neither of us can think of anything to say. Our hearts are heavy, and there's a dark feeling of impending doom looming over us.

I push the soup bowl away. "I'm sorry, Mom. I can't eat. My stomach is in knots."

She nods and picks up the bowl, then sets it in the sink. Without looking at me she says, "I don't know what has happened to Dakota, if anything. But I do know that we have to try and think positively. What my father used to tell me about energy and our hearts has always proven to be true."

"What's that?"

"If you put negative energy out into the world, then you will get negative energy back. The same can be said when we release positive energy."

I slowly shake my head. How the hell am I supposed to think positively right now?

I focus on every nook and cranny on the old ceiling, trying to distract myself from thinking about Dakota, the cop at the lodge, and the look on Dakota's aunt's face. My heart feels heavy and alone. In some ways, I wish I had never been introduced to that beautiful creature. I wouldn't be hurting so badly if I'd not gotten close to her. Dakota is my dream girl—someone I could definitely see spending the rest of my life with. And considering how long it took to meet someone of her quality, odds are I'll never be so fortunate as to know any other girl like her. I need Dakota and I want her back.

By some miracle, I manage to fall asleep. When my mom knocks on my bedroom door, I turn and face the clock. It's 9AM.

"Are you getting up? Everyone involved in the search party will be meeting at the lodge in an hour, so you should get dressed and have a quick coffee now."

I slowly sit up and take a deep breath. I am just sliding into my jeans when my cell rings.

My first thought is that Dakota is calling to tell me that she's all right. However, when I look at the screen, I recognize the Toronto number as James's. "Hello?'

"Hey, buddy. Did I wake you?" His voice is alert and happy.

"I was just getting up. Is everything okay?"

"Everything is more than okay, Ray. I just called to tell you the good news."

"I could definitely use some of that right now. What's up?"

James goes on to tell me about a gig that's just opened up in Toronto. A classy venue. The club is called Rock Empire, and the manager plans on having only A-list bands play there. "I know a guy who worked on the interior design of the place, and he said it's amazing. Big stage, high vaulted ceilings, and lots of cool rock-inspired décor."

"Wow. That sounds great."

"Yeah. And the best news is, we've been asked to open the club as the first act. There's going to be media there and everything. This is really good exposure for us."

"That's crazy. I can't wait." I try to sound upbeat.

"So, whenever you learn the songs—like in a week or so—maybe plan on being back here so the four of us can rehearse. We need to be tight as a group and on our game."

I tell him that I've been too swamped to go over songs since I came back home. I don't want to say anything about my girlfriend being missing. Not yet. "I'll get on the songs you gave me as soon as possible."

We say goodbye and hang up. I'm glad James is excited about the new gig; it sounds amazing. Unfortunately, all my emotions are tied up with Dakota, so getting excited about anything but finding her is impossible.

Mom is sitting at the kitchen table with a piece of paper in front of her. "I guess you and I will be on the same search team today. Joe cancelled because he's got stomach issues."

"I wonder what happened? He seemed fine yesterday."

Mom shrugs. "There is some bad meat going around the rez. Joe may have gotten ill after eating some of it."

"Bad meat? Who the hell would be passing out bad meat?"

"Apparently Butch shot a deer and shared it with a few families. Who knows what was wrong with it."

"Yeah. And something tells me Butch didn't eat any of it himself. What a menace that guy is."

We quickly finish our coffee and are just putting on our boots and coats when there's a soft rap at the door. Mom answers the door to find Mabel standing on the stoop. When she walks in, I can clearly see that she's been crying. Her old eyes are puffy and red, and she has a Kleenex wadded up in one of her hands.

My mother looks alarmed. "What's the matter?"

"I've got some awful news. Can we all sit down?"

The three of us take a seat at the kitchen table. My mother puts her hand on Mabel's shoulder to comfort her.

Mabel takes a breath. "I spoke with the chief a few moments ago, to see about when the search party was going to meet this morning. He told me that there will be no search party until further notice. When I asked him why, he said there's a chance that Dakota has been found."

I sit up straight. "What? Where? Where is she?"

Mabel sniffs. "Harlan wasn't positive it was her. The body in the car was charred very badly. It was brought to the morgue."

My head spins. "What? What body? And what car? A burned body was found inside a car?"

Mabel looks over at me with tears streaming down her face. "You really cared about that girl. Everyone knew that. For your sake, I hope it's not her."

"It's not," I say emphatically. "I feel bad for whomever was found. That's terrible. But it's not Dakota. I'm positive of that."

Mom looks at me. "How can you be sure, son?"

"I don't know. I just think that when you love someone, if something happens to them, you'll feel it. And as much as it's awful that Dakota is missing, I believe that she will be home soon, safe and alive."

Mom's eyes are unsure. "But what about what the chief said? About her personal belongings being found?"

"There can be a very logical reason for that. Like I told you yesterday, she could've lost her backpack or something as simple as that."

Mabel wipes her nose with the tissue. "I hope you're right. But still, there's that matter of the body they found in the car."

"Did they say where they found the car? Was it in Wakeville?"

Mabel shakes her head. "No. That's the weird part. The car was lit on fire out on the logging road, on the way to the landfill."

Instantly, I stop breathing. I remember the car that was under the tarp yesterday while Joe and I were taking that very same road.

I remember what Joe said about the car belonging to the chief's nephew, and how he left it there because the transmission went. Someone must have put a body inside and torched the car. Hopefully, whoever the sadist was, they didn't burn someone alive.

I cross my arms. "I still think we should keep searching for Dakota."

My mother nods in agreement.

Mabel sighs. "There's no real point. The only person around here that was listed as missing was Dakota. Until they can identify who the corpse was, it only makes sense that we hang tight like the chief said."

I stand up. "There's no damn way I'm just sitting around here, waiting for the phone to ring. I'll go nuts."

I pace around the kitchen while Mom picks up the phone and calls the chief. Mabel, still sniffling, puts the kettle on.

I listen to every word of my mother's one-sided conversation with Harlan, but it's mostly things like, "Oh, dear" and "That's terrible."

Finally, she ends the call. After taking a deep breath, she leans back in her chair and looks up at me.

I'm not sure I want to hear the answer. "What?"

"The chief said he's driving Dakota's aunt and cousin to the morgue. They're seeing if there are any discernable features left on the recovered body that might match Dakota's."

"This is bullshit."

"They've got to rule her out, Ray."

Amped up and distraught, I go into my room and shut the door. I quickly grab my drum pad and pull the sticks out of my bag, along with my headphones. After I turn on my laptop, I plug in the flash drive that James gave me with the songs I'm supposed to learn. I scroll to the first track and listen intently, then replay it as I drum along with the music. After I get the first tune down, I move onto the next. Then, once I've got the feel of it, I play along to that one. Sixteen tracks later, my arms feel like they're falling off as I grab a towel and wipe the sweat off my forehead. The tunes I just played are really great, edgy with great tempo. They would be fun to play live.

Mom knocks on the door and offers me something to eat. I try to decline, but she insists, saying I need to keep up my strength. Having no energy to argue, I accept the sandwich and eat quickly, in case I start to think about Dakota again and get queasy. The moment I'm done I return to my room, where I start from track one and go over the whole list of songs again.

After a few hours, Mom comes back and asks me to drive to the lodge so she can talk to the chief about the recovered body. As much as I want to know, there's a big part of me that doesn't.

I must've been practicing for a lot longer than I thought, because as soon as we step outside, I see the red and orange sun pushing its way down over the horizon. We drive to the lodge where, not surprisingly, there are a slew of people gathered at the entrance.

After we cheat park on the road, we get out of the van and join the others. The chatter about the discovered burned body is too much for my head; soon, the talking merges together and all I hear is one solid sound. I feel like I could start screaming as my ears buzz from the gossip.

When it gets too much, I tell Mom that I'm going to the van. "I want to find a better parking space."

I drive around the area numerous times without even looking for a place to park. Instead, I turn on the tunes and zone out.

It's only after I notice Joe getting dropped off at the front of the lodge that I find a place to pull in. Out of all the people gathering, Joe is the only one I want to speak to—especially after learning the news about the body found in the vehicle we spoke about yesterday.

I call his name as I reach the crowd. Immediately he turns around, then walks to me.

I look him over. "I heard you were sick."

"Yeah—I felt like crap last night and this morning, but I'm a bit better now. I heard the crazy news about a body being found, and I had to come down to see if I could find out more."

I nod. "Isn't it weird that the body was found in the vehicle we cruised past on the way to the landfill?

Joe's eyes are wide. "I couldn't believe it. I keep thinking that maybe we should have looked in the car. What if the victim was in there while we were driving past?"

I sigh. "I know, man. It gives me the shivers."

Just then, the wooden front doors to the lodge open. One of the assistants to the chief pokes her head out. "We're going to let people in now. If you all could sit or stand at the far end of the lodge, it will make it easier for the chief to update everyone and answer a few questions."

Joe leans toward me. "Everyone's been saying that they believe the corpse belongs to Dakota. What do you think?"

I shrug. "I'm not sure who the unlucky victim is, but I'm sure it's not Dakota." *At least, it better not be.*

We file into lodge behind everyone else. Once inside, Joe and I blend into the large crowd and wait for Harlan to make his appearance. I zoom in on Mom, who is shoulder to shoulder with Mabel. They both look anxious, their eyes fixated on the chief's office.

When the door opens and the chief appears, a hush falls over everyone. The chief looks distraught. His face is drawn and sallow. Whatever he's about to say to us can't be good.

He clears his throat and puts his shoulders back. He needs to show strength for his people. "Thank you for coming on such short notice. As you all have probably heard by now, a body was found in a car up on the logging road that goes to the landfill. The body was that of a young woman."

Sounds of loud sighs and sympathetic moans ring out from the crowd.

"As you also know, we have a missing young woman from the rez. Most of us have been searching for Dakota Greene. As of yet, we have no concrete information that ties Dakota to the body of the woman found. However, after the police and forensics have done their investigations, they will reach out and let us know."

Mabel raises a hand. "What about the items of Dakota's that were found? Are they running tests on those as well?"

"Yes. The police are being very thorough with their investigations."

My mother yells out next: "What do you suggest we do in the meantime? Are we supposed to sit around and wait? Shouldn't we keep looking for Dakota?"

Harlan shakes his head. "No. As of now, the old logging road is blocked off while the investigators work up there. Also, there will be a lot more police presence on the rez. I'm asking you all to be respectful to these officers."

Joe nudges me. "Why do I get the feeling there's something the chief isn't telling us?"

"It would seem, yes."

* * *

The feeling in the room is heavy and dark. Mabel and Mom are sitting at the table, staring down into their cups of tea. Joe is sitting in the chair in the living room, and I pace back and forth in front of him.

He watches me pace. "I'm sorry you're going through all of this, Ray. I can't imagine how badly you feel right now."

"What I feel is helpless."

"I know, man. I just wish Harlan would've told us everything he knew, instead of holding stuff back."

Mabel, obviously eavesdropping on me and Joe, yells out, "And what about the increased presence on the rez? What are the cops searching for here? I think we, the residents, have a right to know."

"Maybe they think the person who murdered the girl lives on the reservation," Mom chimes in.

Joe nods. "I did notice someone missing from the crowd today. Butch was nowhere to be seen. His cousin was standing behind everyone else, but not Butch. I find that pretty suspicious."

He's right. I hadn't even noticed that Butch wasn't at the lodge, despite almost the entire village being there. That's odd. Unless, of course, he is guilty of something. Maybe that's why the police presence will be amped up. Maybe they're looking for—or monitoring—Butch's movements. He's certainly the first person I'd be looking at.

Then again, he's got an injury to his knee right now. I don't think he'd get too far, unless someone with a vehicle was helping him.

Joe looks thoughtful. "Does anyone know when Butch was released from the jail in Wakeville?"

My mother nods. "Yes. The chief told me he was let out right after Ray was."

I don't want to hear any more. "I'm going to my room." I say goodbye to Mabel and Joe, then quickly make a beeline to my room.

I try to clear my head by sitting on my bed in the quiet, but all I can picture is Dakota. I close my eyes and say a quick prayer that the recently found body isn't hers.

If it is, there's only one person who was motivated to kill her. And if it comes out that Butch is guilty, I will do the same thing to him that he did to her.

If Dakota died by that hands of that monster, I would not rest until I avenge her death. As much as I am pro-life, I will make sure Butch can never hurt anyone ever again.

Joe pushes my door open and sticks his head inside. "You okay, buddy?"

I stand up and straighten my posture. "Yeah. I'm fine. I was just going to do some more practicing to distract myself."

"That's cool. What kind of songs are you going over? Are they any good?"

"They're really good. These guys know their stuff. They really are pro players."

"I guess in your time of grief and worry, at least you have something positive to focus on."

"It's more like a survival thing right now. If I don't do something, I'll go crazy."

Joe asks if he can hear the tracks I've been working on. I pass him the headphones and play the first track for him on my computer.

Right away, I can tell by his expression that he's blown away. When the song is done, he takes off the headphones and looks at me.

"Dude. That was awesome. I can't believe you get to play with these guys."

I shrug. "I wish I gave a shit right now, but honestly, I'd trade the opportunity to play with them for one more day with Dakota. I wish it worked that way. I wouldn't think twice."

"I can understand that, Ray. This whole Dakota thing must really put a damper on all the good fortune you've had recently."

"It doesn't matter. It's not her fault. After all, she was on her way here, to the house, the last time she was seen."

Mom taps on the door. "Are you boys hungry?"

I shake my head. "No. Food is the last thing on my mind right now."

Joe gets up and walks to the door. "I've actually got to be going. But I'll be in touch, Ray. If you need to chat with me, day or night, just call me."

"Thanks, man. I appreciate that."

Even though Joe has had his weirdness with jealousy about me getting the gig, I know him well. Right now, I'm very grateful for his friendship.

* * *

It's 6AM and I've spent the entire night—and first part of the morning—going over songs. My hands have little blisters on them and my arms are killing me. That being said, if it wasn't for the music to lose myself

213

in, I'm sure I would've gone crazy thinking about Dakota.

Lying back on the bed, I pull out my phone and scroll through my old messages. When I get to Dakota's name, I pause, take a deep breath, and open up the messages. My heart sinks as I read our texts to each other. As I scan her words, how much she said that she wanted to be with me, my eyes tear up and my chest tightens. When I can't take any more, I put my phone on the nightstand and roll over onto my side. I breathe through my nose and instantly smell the subtle hint of her hair on my pillow.

Why did it have to be her that went missing? If she did take off somewhere, then for whatever reason couldn't come back right away, I hope she senses how desperately I miss her.

It would be easy for me to just lie here and succumb to the depression, but I can't do that to my mom. I'd worry her to no end. Instead, I've got to do everything I can to fight the way I'm feeling.

Slowly, I will myself to get up and have a shower. Maybe the hot water will perk me up.

I grab a change of clothes and go into the hallway linen closet to grab a towel. I'm just about to step into the bathroom when there's a loud knock on the door.

I look at the clock. It's 8AM. I hope it's not Mabel coming over to chat with Mom.

My mother is emotionally drained and needs her rest right now.

I quickly go to the door before there's another loud knock. I unlock the deadbolt and open the door. It takes me a second to comprehend who is standing in front of me. It's the chief, with two of the ladies that work at the lodge.

"Hi, Harlan. What brings you here this early?"

"Is your mom home? I need to speak with both of you."

I invite them in, then go to my mother's room and gently knock on her door. "Mom. Get up. The chief is here."

It's a moment before she answers. "Why is Harlan here at this time in the morning?"

"I'm not sure, but he wants to speak with us."

I turn and walk back to the front room while Mom gets ready. "What's going on, Harlan? Is this about the girl's body that was found?"

Mom walks up behind me, wearing her housecoat and slippers. She briefly says hello to everyone, then asks them if they want tea or coffee. Nobody does. The chief asks her to have a seat. "There's important information that I need to share."

The three unexpected guests sit on the couch and I drag two chairs from the kitchen for me and Mom to sit on. Once Harlan has our undivided attention, he says, "As you

215

know, there was a body of a young girl found burned in a car up on the landfill road."

My mother nods. "Yes. We were at the lodge when you told everyone."

"Well, the police and investigators called me early this morning. They have made an identification on the girl."

"Who was it? Was it someone from another reserve? Or was she a white girl?"

Harlan slowly shakes his head. "I'm sorry to say, Ray. It was neither."

A hard lump grows in my throat, and my chest feels like there's a dozen people standing on it. "Who was she, chief?" I'm unable to take my eyes off his.

"It was Dakota, wasn't it?" my mother whimpers.

Slowly, Harlan nods his head.

"What do you mean? It can't be her. You're wrong! The cops and the medical people probably didn't even try to identify the body. They just assumed that since Dakota was missing, it had to be her."

"I'm sorry, Ray. I know you two were close. But Dakota's dental records match the body found in the burning car. There's no mistake. It's her."

My mom turns to me. "I'm so sorry, son. I know how deeply you cared for her."

I stand. "This isn't happening. This isn't the way her story is supposed to end. She was too young and too special. She can't be gone. She just can't be." I wipe the tears from my eyes. "Why her?"

"Have the police arrested anyone yet?" Mom asks.

"Not as of yet. But I'm fully confident that they—"

"Why the hell don't they question Butch?" I holler. "That's who did it!"

Harlan gives me a look of sympathy. "They can't just arrest someone without having all the evidence together first, Ray. It doesn't work that way."

"Have they even questioned the piece of shit yet?"

Harlan looks at the floor. "They can't."

"Why the hell not?" My voice is growing even louder.

"Well, because he seems to have vanished into thin air."

"Are you serious? This is ridiculous. The whole reason they can't find him is because he's fucking guilty and doesn't want to go to jail, so he split. That bastard is probably halfway to Vancouver by now. He could hide out for years."

"Don't jump the gun, Ray. It can't have made it far."

"This is so stupid. Have they even put out an APB on him yet?"

"No. He's only wanted for questioning at this point, not for murder. I'm sure if they can't find him soon, or if any crucial evidence is found, then they'll most likely put out an APB."

"I can't believe I'm hearing this. Dakota is dead, who knows how horrifying and painful her last moments of life were, and the only likely person that killed her is roaming out there free."

"I know you're upset, Ray. But I promise you that all is being done to get to the truth of what happened."

All eyes are on me as I pace back and forth. "I can't just do nothing. If the cops can't find Butch, maybe I can."

Mom stands and walks over to me, then grabs my shoulders and looks me in the eye. "You'll do no such thing, Ray. Now, I'm sorry about what has happened, you know I am. I cared for her, too. But if you think you're leaving this house to go running around searching for Butch and causing more upset on the rez, you're sadly mistaken. I need you to be strong right now. I need you to trust that all the professionals are on this case and will do what needs doing to solve it. Do not make everything worse by meddling around the village and getting in the way."

Her eyes are severe as she looks into mine. I can tell that she's very serious. I think the fact that I just got released from jail because Butch and I were fighting has pushed her too far.

"You will stay here with me, son. And we'll get through this together."

Harlan and the two women stand up and walk to the door. "I'm sorry, folks," the chief says. "I was dreading this visit. I was really hoping I could tell everyone it wasn't Dakota." He puts his head down. "We have to go. We'll be stopping at every house to inform people of the latest news. Again, Ray. I am so sorry. If you feel you need someone to talk with, please, give me a call."

Once the three are well on their way to the neighbors' house, Mom walks up and wraps her arms around me. "It's going to be okay, eventually, son. The pain will fade and life will go on. I know it's hard to see that right now, but I promise you, the pain will fade."

I let out a sob. "I don't think I will ever get over how badly this hurts. How can I? She was perfect, Mom. And we were going to be together."

"I know, Ray. I know."

* * *

It's a few hours later, and all I've heard—despite lying on my bed with the pillow over my face to block the noise out—are the knocks on the door and the sounds of people talking and crying. At one point, Mom came to my room and told me Joe was in the house. He came to see if I was okay. I told my mother I had no desire to see anyone, so she told him to leave.

When the voices eventually fade and I hear the door shut for the last time, Mom knocks on my bedroom door and opens it. "Here, Ray. I made you a cup of tea." I hear her place the cup on the bedside table, then walk out of the room, closing my door gently behind her.

I feel somewhat guilty for succumbing to my pain. She needs me, and I am the man of the house. I should be acting strong for her. But I can't. It hurts too much.

Chapter 14

The night passes slowly as I stare out the window. Usually, the skies here are clear and the stars are shining brightly, but not tonight. There are dark, rolling clouds churning overhead, reflecting the way I'm feeling—dark and angry.

Mom goes out alone after repeatedly trying to get me to go with her, but I can't. My head feels light and strange and my body feels as though it's been filled with lead.

After a couple of hours, Mom comes back. She comes into my room and sits at the bottom of the bed, then proceeds to tell me everything that happened while she was out. I retain about half of it. Most was about how there are three or four cops in the village, all with some purpose on the rez. A couple were asking around about Butch, seeing if anyone knew where he was.

Then Mom said that she ran into Dakota's aunt, who said that Dakota's diary had recent entries about Butch, and how afraid she was of him ("One day, I know he's going to get me.") Then Mom ran into Harlan and learned that the police are worried about Butch coming after me and Joe, after the cop station received an anonymous call, with a voice whispering, "Revenge is sweet," before hanging up.

I told Mom I wasn't worried. "If that murderous bastard shows up, I'll take him out."

"Don't be foolish, son. Never fight anyone crazier that you. Butch is definitely crazier."

* * *

The next day passes slowly. Other than getting up to use the bathroom, I've stayed in bed. Mom has come into my room numerous times to put food on my nightstand, but I leave the tray untouched. I don't feel hungry or thirsty. In fact, if it wasn't for the pain my heart is in, I'd feel nothing at all.

I can hear Mabel and Mom chatting in the front room but can't make out what they're saying. Then, when the clock reads midnight, I hear Mabel say good night to Mom. A few seconds later, I hear both Mom and Mabel scream.

Instantly I bolt out of bed and sprint to the front room, where I see the two women looking freaked out, their hands over their mouths. Mabel sees me, then points through the open door to the darkness outside. "It's awful. Who would do such a thing?"

I motion Mom and Mabel to come away from the door. By the look on their faces, I know whatever is outside must be bad. I slide on my shoes, then grab the flashlight from the shelf.

When I'm on the top step outside the door, I turn the flashlight on and shine it on the ground. Immediately, I see the horrifying sight that terrified my mother and Mabel. A small, furry creature is lying on its back, a slit running from its throat all the way down to its belly. Its entrails have been pulled out and its snout has been duct-taped closed.

Slowly I step closer, until I identify the creature as a puppy. It couldn't have been more than six months old. I sigh deeply, then grab the pup by one of its legs and pull it away from where Mabel will need to walk on her way home. I cover the dead animal with an old piece of dirty fabric I find near the corner of the house.

Once back inside, I join Mom and Mabel in the living room. Both women are visibly distraught and shaking. Mom looks up at me with wet eyes. "We need to call the police and tell them what was left in front of our house."

"It can wait until tomorrow. Otherwise we'll be up all night giving statements."

I walk Mabel home and tell her to call if she sees or hears anything. When I'm back at home, it takes a good hour of sitting with Mom until she's calm enough to go to bed.

Once alone, I sit on the sofa and think about that poor puppy, and how horrible his last minutes of life must have been. And I know there's only one monster who has proven himself evil enough to do such a thing.

I guess Butch figured, since it's nighttime and there aren't any cops around, he could come out of hiding and continue his reign of terror.

I shut the lights off, then double check the windows and door to make sure everything is locked. I just make it to the doorway of my bedroom when my cellphone, which has been sitting on the nightstand, lights up. Someone is calling me this late at night.

I walk over and pick up the phone. Joe's number flashes on the screen. I pick up. "Hello. Why are you calling me at 1:30 in the morning?"

"Trust me. It's important." He sounds panicked. "I had to call."

"What's up?"

"It's Butch. He's been spotted on the rez tonight. My cousin was driving home from Wakeville about an hour ago, and he saw Butch with a hunting knife strapped to his side, walking near your place,"

"I'm not surprised, considering the twisted gift he just left out front." I describe the mutilated puppy.

"That's horrid. What a disgusting piece of shit." He pauses. "I also heard something else, earlier tonight. I was going to tell you about it in the morning."

"What's that?"

"I heard the reason the cops are on the rez is because they found jerry cans in a shed outside the house Butch was staying at. The cops said to the chief that they have other evidence that connects Butch to the car fire."

"Like what?"

"I'm not sure. My cousin wasn't told anything about that."

"All right, well, there's nothing we can do about it tonight so—"

"Listen, Ray. I really think Butch is going to try to take you out before he disappears for good. I left you something, a few minutes ago. I couldn't bring it to your door because of your mom, so I ran down and put it near the dumpster at the side of your house."

"What is it?"

"It's a piece. I thought, in case Butch tried to get into your house under the cover of darkness, at least you'd have something to protect you and your mom with."

"Joe. Thanks, man, But I don't want a weapon like that in the house, and my mother wouldn't, either."

"Don't be dumb, Ray. Would you rather Butch killed you both, then got away? Look at what he's done so far to Dakota and how he gutted that little pup. It's not a matter of *if* Butch will try and do you in, it's a matter of *when*. Besides, you can't leave the piece outside. What if a kid finds it in the morning?"

I shake my head. "Fine. I'll go and get it. But in the morning, you're coming here to pick it up. Now, where exactly is it?"

"It's wrapped in a t-shirt between the dumpster and your house. And...Ray?"

"What?"

"Be careful."

Once Joe is off the phone, I go to my closet and rifle around until I find my bat. Then I put on my hoodie and quietly walk to the front door.

* * *

My hands are shaking as I grip the bat. I slowly open the front door, kick off my trainers, then walk barefoot into the shadows that lead around back to the alley. My heart is pounding so quickly, I can feel the pulse in my jaw.

I step gently on the cold ground. If Butch is waiting for me in the darkness, the last thing I want to do to make a sound. It's the same reason I didn't bring the flashlight.

It's pitch dark in the alleyway beside my house. I take small, slow steps toward the dumpster. Once there, I take a hand off the bat and reach until I touch metal, then use the dumpster as a guide as I feel my way to the edge and around the other side. I bend down and search in the dark for the gun wrapped in the t-shirt but can't locate it.

Then, there's a quick burst of light behind me. My heart just about leaps out of my chest as I whirl around and raise my bat. "If that's you, Butch, you'd better get the hell out of here."

"It's not there, Ray."

"What? What isn't?"

"The gun."

The flash happens again, this time revealing a face. Only, it's not who I thought it was. It's not Butch. In disbelief, I look harder. "Joe? Is that you?"

"Of course it's me, you stupid ass. It's always been me."

"What are you talking about."

Joe takes a step closer. "I'm talking about how you took everything from me. That now it's my turn to finish what I started and take everything from you."

My eyes are getting used to the dark surroundings, but as soon as the lighter Joe is holding flicks off again, everything plunges to blackness.

"Joe. Have you lost your mind? What the hell are you doing?"

Joe laughs, and I hear the unmistakable sound of a gun cocking. "Goodbye, Ray."

I'm frozen in place. The only thing I can do is close my eyes and wait.

But then, I hear another voice. A very familiar one.

"Run, Ray," Butch says.

And the gun goes off.

I can't see a thing, but just after the shot rings out, I hear a mad scuffle. Joe and Butch are fighting.

I don't know what to do. No matter how hard I will my legs to move, they wont. I'm frozen with fear. It's not until the second gunshot goes off that my legs unfreeze.

I'm turning to get away when I'm hit by what feels like a steamroller as both men land on top of me. My head slams against the side of the house, and I feel myself losing consciousness. Slowly, my limp body slides down the wall.

* * *

When I come to, Harlan is standing above me, shining a penlight on my face. My voice is raspy and weak. "Harlan. What happened? Did Joe kill Butch?'

He shakes his head.

"Did someone get shot?"

"Butch was trying to protect you. He got the gun away from Joe. In the scuffle, Joe was shot."

"Is my mom okay?"

"She's fine. Just a bit shaken up." Harlan takes off his jacket, rolls it up, and puts it under my head. "Hang in there, Ray. The ambulance will be here soon."

"Y'know, Chief, I could never have dreamed that Joe was the one who murdered Dakota. He must've been hiding how twisted he was, all these years."

Harlan nods. "I think you getting that Toronto gig really pushed him over the edge."

"I should have known something was wrong when he and I were driving on the old logging road and spotted your nephew's car. I wanted to look inside, and he told me not to bother."

Harlan gives me a funny look. "Wait a minute. What are you talking about? That car didn't belong to my nephew. The car was Joe's. The same one he reported missing."

As I look into the chief's eyes, my mind rewinds to the drive to the landfill. I stopped right behind that car. I wanted to take the tarp off and look inside, but Joe dissuaded me. If only I hadn't listened to him.

Maybe I could have found Dakota while she was still alive. Tears roll down my cheeks.

Harlan shakes his head slowly. "Ray, if you're wondering if you could have saved her that day, you couldn't have. From what I understand, she was dead long before she was carried to the car."

I take a deep breath. "She wasn't burned alive?"

"No. I just got an update a few hours ago. She was strangled, and her body was put in the trunk before the car was lit on fire."

Epilogue

The bright orange harvest moon takes up half the sky as we file into the shiny black SUV. Tonight is going to be wild, with thirty thousand people expected to be at the auditorium—our biggest show yet. With TV interviews and terrific sales with our music, this band is on fire.

If I'd stayed on the rez, wallowing in sorrow over the loss of my beautiful Dakota, I don't think I would've survived. Thankfully, mom made me go back to Toronto and keep my position as the drummer in this band. Since then, I've slowly been able to work through my grief.

Sometimes, when we're on stage and the crowd is cheering and loving us, I think of Joe and how he would've given his left nut to be a part of this lifestyle. But his jealousy ate him like a disease and caused him to do unspeakable things. Now, he's probably stuck between the spirit world and this world, tormented and in anguish.

Not that my heart breaks for him. Why should it? He took Dakota away from this world, and from all the people who loved her. I only feel pity for Joe now.

As for Butch, I couldn't be prouder of him. Before, he was a chronic alcoholic with anger problems and definitely someone who burned every bridge. Fast-forward to today, and he's a whole new guy. He went through rehab and now, when he's not in his anger management sessions, he's working at the lodge with the chief, helping to council kids about the dangers of alcohol. Mom has been letting him stay at the house in my old room, since I'm on the road so much and don't use it.

At first I was nervous about him being there with her, in case he had a relapse, but he put my mind at ease with everything good he's been doing. Yesterday, Mom called and told me how she and Mabel are focussing their efforts on raising more awareness for missing and murdered Indigenous women. Apparently, Butch told them that he would like to get involved and help in whatever way he can. I guess miracles can happen.

As for me, I'm finally happy in my skin. With everything that's happened, I've realized that success isn't going to make me happy and content in the long run. My happiness needs to come from within. So, every morning when I wake up, I remind myself that even if this awesome band I'm in dissolved tomorrow, I am still worthful.

I keep the eagle feather my mother gave me tied to my drum kit. No matter what happens down the road, I will find my place in this world, on the rez or off. I will stay firm-footed on my journey and will always stand proudly as a Cree.

The End

* * *

Lance grew up in Nepean, Ottawa, where he lived with his father, Rae Chalmers, an accomplished singer and musician, and his mother, Anne Chalmers, an employee at The Indigenous Bar Association in Ottawa. From a young age, Lance was exposed to music; he soon followed in his father's footsteps and developed a passion to play music, primarily the drums. Since then, he has mastered his craft and played in many iconic bands.

Lance has been featured on TV shows such as, *It's a Living, This Hour Has 22 Minutes*, and *The West Coast Music Awards*. In 2023, Lance was inducted into the Canadian Music Hall of Fame with the iconic Canadian classic rock band, Trooper. He currently resides in BC, where he teaches guitar, bass, and drums. On weekends, Lance plays gigs with numerous bands, and is often commissioned as a session percussionist for various artists worldwide. An avid reader and blogger, Lance looks forward to adding *author* to his long list of artistic endeavors.

BWL Publishing
bwlpublishing.ca